Dedicati

Firstly I want to thank Jehovah for blessing me with the ability to tell stories. Without him, none of the things I've accomplished would've been possible. I would love to give thanks to my Mother, Tara Lipscomb for always supporting me in anything I do. My Aunt Timea for always pushing me to reach any goals I set for myself. My sister Desiree, although we fight every day, for making sure I excel in everything. She's a motivation. My Ace, Ashley Harris, for making sure I kept my head in the books during my last year of High School. My grandma Mommy for making sure I let everyone know about my books. My promoter! My bestfriend Damonte, you was up listening to these stories come to fruition.

And thank you to all my readers who spent time and money on my books. I appreciate all the love and support. With any of your support, none of this would have happened. Miss Jenkins you are a hero of mine for simply being a shoulder I could lean on & talk too at one of the lowest points of my life. Because of you, I've learned so much about myself and the strength and passion I have to conquer my dreams. I'm forever indebted to the support you've shown me.

Also by Bronchey (Ju'Tone Sair) Battle

Billionaire Boyz

Gangsta' Bitch: The Mei'Yari Lewis Story

Seduced by The Hustle

Seducing The Hustle

Gangsta: The Sair Lewis Story

Coming Soon!

Exquisite Nights

Contact

Twitter: *@Bronchey_Battle*

Instagram: *@__jutone__*

Facebook: *Bronchey Battle*

Chapter One

2008

Walking in the house I found my mother sprawled out on the kitchen floor. There was a bottle of Taaka Vodka in one hand while she puffed on an almost finished cigarette in the other. Looking around the dirty cramped apartment we stayed in, located in the Hunters Point projects in San Francisco, I shook my head in disgust as I headed for my room.

Bypassing my mom on the floor, I took a second look at her. Her once jet black curls that spiraled to the middle of her back were now thin and straggly looking. Her once glowing high yellow complexion had now taken on an ashy look. The beautiful curves that she once possessed were now a pile of chicken bones. The sparkle behind her hazel eyes had now dimmed. The once envied Queen to the *King of the streets* had fallen victim to the environment that surrounded her life.

Shaking my head, I stepped over her and went into my room. Picking up boxers, jeans, and t-shirts, I began cleaned the dungeon I called my room. Picking up my sneakers to put them back in their boxes, I could hear my mom calling me from the living room.

Dropping my shoes on the floor, I opened the door to my room to see what she wanted.

"What?" I asked, standing in the doorway that led to the living room.

"You've grown to become a smart, intelligent, and handsome young man HaKoda. If your Daddy was still here, booooy it'd be something crazy," She said, looking at me as if she hadn't seen me in years.

"Thanks ma." I responded, turning back around to go into my room.

"I'M NOT FINISHED TALKING TO YOU HaKoda! AND SINCE YOU WANNA BE DISRESPECTFUL BY WALKING AWAY WHILE I'M STILL TALKING, I GOT SOME WORDS FOR YO MU'FUCKIN ASS. You need to start bringing some more money up in here. I'm getting up there in age and I can't continue doing the shit I been doing to make money so you need to get out there and do something."

"Look ma. I'm not trying to hear 'bout none of dat shit you be doing. I bring what I can in here from working at the barbershop and I'm doing that underhanded. I'm seventeen and shit but damn. I'm making about $600 a month and I'm giving you half. What else do you need from me?"

"More NIGGA!"

"If Dad was still here you wouldn't be on me like this. But since you checked outta life after he passed, you just don't give a fuck? GET YO JUNKIE ASS OFF THAT SHIT YOU SMOKING, AND THERE'D BE MORE MONEY IN THIS MOTHA'FUCKA. Uncle Ahmed pays the rent out this raggedy mu'fucka, and you get a SSI check every month."

After having to pretty much raise myself after my Dad died, I'd lost the majority of respect I held for my mother. She let the drugs turn her out, and it cost her, our relationship. I love my Mother more than life, but I hold so much resentment towards her.

"Check this out nigga. Regardless of how you feel, this raggedy mu'fucka is mine! And you're going to watch your mouth talking to me like that. I am still your mama!!"

"Act like it then."

"I'm going to say this and then I'm done." She said, getting in my face. I stood at 6'1'' towering over her 5'5'' frame. "I'm giving you until the first of next month to start bringing in some more money or you can get the fuck out of my spot."

"So, what, you gon' put me out?"

"I sure the fuck am! I want a thousand dollars by the first."

"That's two weeks."

"Make it happen. You better have Ahmed snake ass give it too you!"

She rolled her eyes hard and turned on her heels. Scratching at her arms hard, she drew blood as she slammed the door shut to her room. I knew that if I didn't get my cake up, I'd be homeless.

It wasn't even about bringing money in here to help out. She wanted more money so I could help feed her habit. Although I refrained from entering *The Game*, the only way I'd be able to bring in a *G* a month is Hustlin'.

"What's good nephew?" my Uncle Ahmed asked, as we dapped hands.

"Nothing man."

"C'mon nephew. You know I know you better than that. What's going on?" he asked, taking a seat at his kitchen table. Uncle Ahmed was the definition of an old school player. Hustling major weight back in the day for my Dad, he inherited the Empire. My Dad asked him to make him one promise before he died. However, he hadn't. He wasn't taking care of us. He took the money he used from his illegal activities and opened up a few businesses around the area.

Sporting a short fade, with diamonds in both ears.

He's clearly living with no worries, but we're out here struggling. It's a Cold World. After it went down that day at the court house, Unc Ahmed was now a retired from the streets.

"I need a plug man. Shit getting hectic and I need some real paper coming through, you feel me?"

"HaKoda, I haven't taken you under my wing the way I want to is because I know you to be a lot smarter than the average nigga your age. You fought the allure of the game after everything went down at the trial. You're too good for the streets. It's in your blood, but it's not for you. What has you chasing the life all of a sudden?" He quizzed, giving me his undivided attention.

"It's a long story that I don't feel like getting into right now. Is there anybody you know that's looking for a worker? It's important."

"What if I give you a raise?"

"Check this out Unc, unless you trying to throw a couple bands to ya' boi every month, there isn't much you can do but to help me get in touch with somebody that can put me on." I responded as respectfully as I could. Resorting to this life was not my ideal lifestyle choice, but my Moms left no alternative.

"I'll see what I can do." He responded, just as a black BMW M3 pulled up in front of the house. My mouth was drooling as I lusted over the beautiful automobile.

"Whose whip is that?" I waited to see who was going to get out the car.

"My young nigga La'Ron. Actually, he might be the man to help you with your situation."

"With a whip like that, shit I hope so," I commented as I watched Ahmed head out front to meet La'Ron.

Once I get on my feet, imma have my shit just like that, I thought.

Uncle Ahmed hit me with some news that La'Ron was willing to work me ONLY off the strength him. I jumped head first into the game without the proper knowledge or grooming.

I was like a mouse in a cage full of snakes. Reputation to be known, La'Ron was a crazy nigga that didn't play when it came to business and money. I had to be on my shit.

Chapter Two

Pittsburg High, *the home of the Pirates*. My stomping grounds.

Making a transaction right before my eyes, I watched from afar as Dammar made his sell on the corner of School Street. Dapping hands, they exchanged the drugs and money. They did it so smoothly, to the untrained eye, they looked as if they were just showing each other love.

"What's poppin' wit my nigga HaKoda?" He asked walked towards me?

Standing at the Creative Arts building stairs, we dapped hands.

Dressed in black True Religion jeans, and a black short sleeve button up, he was fresh. The Air Jordan 12 playoffs were on his feet. Freshly faded haircut accompanied with enough waves to make a sea sick.

"Same shit different day. I can't call it." I responded, as I watched his customer head down the steps to join the crowd of students entering the school.

I didn't have the most money in the world, but one thing I never slacked on was my apparel. A pair of black Levi jeans on my ass, a short sleeve Burberry button up courtesy of the local booster, and black suede Timberlands on my feet.

My shoulder length dreads were braided into a Mohawk going to the back of my head. Caramel complexion with a single dimple in my left cheek.

Hazel eyed nigga with light freckles, standing 6'1"
at the age of 17.

"So word around town is, niggas finna start
fuckin wit La'Ron. What's good?"

"Who you hear dat shit from?"

Dammar and I had grown up together, and were
pretty cool although he slung that shit and I
didn't. Him being a dope boy and me being a
straight-laced student, we had different views on
life. He knew of my situation at home, and had
even looked out for me a few times.

"C'mon bruh, you know mu'fuckas talk."

"Nah bro, it ain't nothing too serious. Just
some slight shit."

"Yeah whatever nigga, just be safe. If you
need anything, you already know."

"I'm already knowing" I replied, dapping hands with him as the school bell signaled our moment of departure.

When that *3:03pm* bell rang, I couldn't sprint out of Miss Jenkins English class fast enough! Time wasn't necessarily on my side, and the faster I linked up with La'Ron, the better.

Walking to *Angelo's* off Harbor St, I noticed La'Ron's Benz driving towards the store.

All the hoes from the school went flocking.

 Rolling the window down, he looked straight at me. "Hop in bro."

Without hesitation, I jumped into the front seat. All eyes were on us as he turned his music up. *"Fuck U Gon Do 'Bout It"* by Plies was blaring out the speakers.

"I'll check you later," I hollered to Dammar as we sped off. My body melted into the soft peanut leather seats as we hit the streets.

"So I hear you looking to be put on." La'Ron said, keeping his eyes on the road. Looking from the Rolex on his wrist, and the diamonds glistening in his ears, I was certain he could teach me a thing or two.

"I am. I need this shit bad too."

"Yo Uncle told me a lil about ya situation at the house with your Moms. I had that exact situation, so I see where the motivation to *get it* is coming from."

His eyes left the road as he looked me over.

"Yeah its crazy man, but I gotta get it the best way I can." I said, looking him dead in the eye.

"I hear you bruh, I definitely do. But ya Unc also let it be known, you're very intelligent and you're better than these streets. So what I'm going to do is make you my cash handler. What that entails is you going to pick up my dough from around the city and bring it to me. Nothing too crazy."

"Good looking." I responded.

The conversation slowly died after that. Plaguing me, I asked, "How old are you man?" Judging by his looks, dude could only be a few years older than me. He had a short tapered fro, chocolate complexion, and a goatee.

"Nineteen."

"Oh okay cool."

"I'm going to have you start working tomorrow."

"Perfect." And just like that, a hustler was born.

Chapter Three

It's been a week since La'Ron picked me up from the school and I was making moves. Standing in the foyer of his condo, I handed La'Ron the money I picked up from his corner boys.

"What's the count from the crew running *Woods Manor*?" He was looking through the Gucci duffle bag filled with money.

"Sixty bands from them niggas, and its *$420,000* total." I responded.

"You counted this shit?" He asked, looking me in the eyes as he stood from the table.

"Three times while there just to make sure it was all good."

"That's what the fuck I'm talking about," he said, smacking my hand after every word, "You a natural bruh. I've heard stories about ya Pop's and how he used to run shit back in the day. It's in you! You quick on your feet and you listen. I see it!"

I nodded my head in appreciation, not knowing how to respond.

"I talked to ya Uncle earlier bro, I told him you won't be working at the shop no more."

I looked at that nigga like he was crazy, before I finally spoke up. "Fuck you do that for? I need that money bruh!"

"Working for me makes you a target my nigga!"

Calming down, I took in his words. "I hear what you saying bro, but I have a due date on some cake that I DO NOT HAVE!"

"The money don't seem like a problem lil bruh. Niggas be dressed in Burberry and shit," he jokingly responded.

I burst out laughing.

"By time I'm done with you, you gone have everything you need. I'm finna have you, *Seducing The Hustle.*"

"All dat shit sounds cool, but that money I'm making at the shop is the only thing keeping me afloat. I got some shit going on at the house and I need to have a few thousand in my hands by the 1st or else I'll be assed the fuck out."

Reaching in his pocket, La'Ron handed me a knot of one hundred dollar bills. "That's four racks right there. I know how shit be when parents be on that shit."

"I been working for you for a lil minute now, and everything is cool but I don't feel comfortable taking handouts," I said, putting the money back in his hands, "I like to work for what I feel I deserve so in the long run, I won't be indebted to nobody. Pops always taught me that shit."

A huge grin spread across his face as he listened to me talk.

"Why you cheesin?"

"I like where your head is at man. You smart and you have the makings of becoming something bigger than this. Guaranteed! And just for not accepting the money, I really want you to keep it bruh. Consider it an advance on your first weeks pay. "

Can't argue with that, I thought.

"You ready to go on your first mission with me?" He asked, headed towards his garage.

"Yup," I responded as I hopped in the front seat of his black Range Rover.

I dozed off in the truck, and when I awoke, we were in the Sunnydale part of San Francisco. "What we doing out here?"

"Collecting some money and work."

"You want me to roll in there with you or stay out here."

"You can roll in there with me."

Reaching over me before hopping out the truck, he went into the glove compartment. He grabbed a .45 and handed it to me. "Gotta be prepared for anything, you know what to do if the time comes."

Although I was new to the game, I wasn't new to holding guns. Growing up with a King Pin for a Father, guns were a everyday thing.

I hopped out the truck wearing a black Hollister hoodie, black Levi jeans, and black Jordan 13's. I followed La'Ron lead as we walked towards the house. He was dressed in a red Ralph Lauren polo, white True Religion jeans, and some clean ass Gucci sneakers.

Knocking on the door of the house, I threw the hood of my sweater on my head. Walking inside the house, I kept my hand wrapped around the trigger of the gun. The pungent smell of weed was all around the house. There were two other dudes in the room aside from the one who opened the door.

I kept my back to the wall so I could be in clear view of my surroundings. An eerie feeling had crept over me, and I couldn't shake it.

"Where my shit at?" La'Ron asked, one of the dudes who was seated on the rundown brown couch in the middle of the room.

"Man that shit you gave us was straight garbage!"

"Nigga quit playing with me. If my shit was garbage, run it back."

Yellow nigga La'Ron was arguing with stood from the couch and paced the floor.

This being the first time I've been in the middle of some shit like this, I was on high alert.

"I don't have shit to give you," Yellow dude finally yelled out.

"Run dat bread then bruh," La'Ron said, remaining calm.

Looking around the room, I noticed a black duffle bag tucked in the corner. My instincts was on too everything in the room, and I was certain the money was in there.

Continuously scanning the room, my eyes zeroed in on the dark skin dude who opened the door. He was discreetly reaching in the waistband of his jeans.

Without hesitation I pulled my gun from the inside of my sweater and let off two rounds in between his eyes.

BAM! BAM!

Without hesitation, La'Ron pulled out his 9mm and aimed it at the two dudes in the living room. Sprinting to the corner where the duffle bag was, I grabbed it up and walked back to the door also pointing my gun at the two.

"You niggas was trying to set me up?" La'Ron yelled, shaking his gun from one dude to the other.

While ranting, another nigga came from the back of the house with a shotgun.

BOOM! BOOM!

The door exploded behind my head where he aimed. Diving on the floor, I squeezed the trigger, shooting him in the knee as the other two niggas reached for their guns. La'Ron hit yellow nigga in the head, brains spraying everywhere.

Dark skin nigga that occupied the couch was able to reach his gun and they began trading shots. Letting another round into the nigga with the shotgun, I rocked him to sleep forever.

Crouching from my position, I shot at dark skin, buying La'Ron and I enough time to haul ass out of the house. Duffle bag in tow, we sprinted to the Range.

"HURRY UP NIGGA!" I yelled. La'Ron was fumbling with the keys trying to unlock the door. I hopped in the passenger seat as the window was shot out.

BAM!

Dark skin was letting off rounds into the back of the truck. Hopping in the front seat, La'Ron put the keys in the ignition and sped off leaving tire marks on the ground.

What the fuck just happened? I thought as La'Ron drove to a Public storage unit in Richmond.

45 minutes later we pulled up. Unlocking the padlock to his unit, he opened it, revealing a black

1970 Dodge Charger R/T and a 2008 black on black Dodge Charger R/T on 22's.

"These you?" I asked.

"Yeah, these my under cars. I want you to have the '08 and Imma take the '70. Hold on to that money we and take it to your hut. I'm about to head to Oakland to lay low for a minute. I want you to run *The Baileys* bruh. As of tomorrow, make it do what it do. If it's any bricks in there, you're entitled to two." Handing me the keys, he dapped me up, saying "Good looking out for ya boy."

Grabbing the duffle bag out the backseat of the bullet ridden Range Rover, I hopped in the Charger and sped off. The events of what transpired replayed in my head over and over as I headed to the house to get a nights rest.

Chapter Four

Finding the right soldiers that were hungry to be put on, I was ecstatic. Standing before the group of five, I had the perfect team of niggas. Calico, dark skin and lanky that was good at cutting and bottling coke. The nigga was quick on his feet and stayed on point at all times.

CripCrip; he was the A-Wax from *Menace II Society* of the crew. Stayed with the hammer on e'm, ready for whatever, but talked the most shit. Nigga kept his hair in rollers, but was quick with the pistol. He'd be my shooter.

Kasey, a brown skin medium built kid, would serve as an enforcer. The muscle that'd shoot first and handle what comes next afterwards. Known for his ruthlessness, I knew he'd be an asset to the team. Dammar served as my right hand.

A cloud of weed smoke filled the air as they passed the backwoods around the room.

"All you niggas know why y'all here," I started, looking them each in the eye as I scanned the room, "we all hungry. I'm offering you niggas a chance to eat, and I mean WELL. Everybody knows their role, so let's get to work."

"Calico, since you fastest at cutting this shit, I'm going to need you to get started ASAP." Dammar said, already knowing what to do.

"All you niggas are going to pinch in. We going to cut this shit into twenties. I'll meet y'all in the Laundromat," I said, as they filed out of the rented apartment.

Walking into the parking lot of the low income housing complex, I popped the trunk of my Charger and removed the *Gucci* back pack and bottle of *Clorox* bleach. In a worst case scenario, I planned on washing all evidence away in the machines.

"I'm not helping you niggas cut this shit up, but I'll be here to make sure nothing goes wrong. If something goes awry, I want y'all to dump that shit in them machines, and pour bleach over it. If cop's run through here, they won't find shit. Feel me?" I had a seat on one of the machines.

"Let's get this shit popping." Calico said, already bottling up.

After a couple hours we were ready to open up shop. Fiends started flocking as the buzz about my product started making its way around the apartment complex. Seeing all the money coming in, I was like a kid on Christmas.

Looking out of the window at the other dealers scattered throughout the complex, we were taking all of their clientele.

These niggas aint gone have a choice but to start selling my shit, I thought.

For hours, fiends from all over Pittsburg were requesting our services. It was going on *2:00am* and I was ready to get the fuck out the hood. As I was making my exit, I noticed three hooded figures creeping behind an incoming car.

Alerting the crew of the impending gun battle, I withdrew my .357 magnum out of the waistband of the white *Dickies* shorts I wore. I was ready to get it popping.

CripCrip hit the lights just as one of the guys kicked in the door. Pulling a sawed-off, double barreled shotgun from out of the washing machine he was working next to, Kasey aimed.

BOOM! BOOM! BOOM!

The first guy fell dead instantly. Living for moments like this, Kasey was in his element.

Calico, spotting another dude circling around the building stood near the door. As the dude rushed in, Calico popped him. His body made a loud thud on the tile floor. His blood painted the floor.

There is one left. I stood to look out of the window and bullets rained inside. Diving onto the ground, I rolled underneath the table.

"I'm hit!" Kasey yelled out.

Rolling from underneath the table, just the door flew open. Aiming my weapon, I shot the nigga in the stomach, bringing him to his knees. Eye level, I shot him between the eyes, blood decorating my face as his body thudded on the ground.

"Get that nigga and get the fuck outta here!" I ordered as Calico carried Kasey to his 2001 orange Camaro SS.

Grabbing all the money and remainder of the drugs, I raced to my car and high tailed the fuck outta there.

This is the cost of *Seducing The Hustle*, I thought racing down Bailey Road.

Chapter Five

I woke up in a deep sweat. Panting heavily, I raced into the bathroom and ran cold water onto my face towel. Washing my face, I let the water drench me.It had been a week since shit popped off in *The Baileys* and I was on high alert at all times.

I'm not gone be able to go back to sleep, I thought. Walking in my room I picked up my brown T-Mobile Sidekick LX to check the time. *4:04am* it read.

Walking over to the loose floor board in my closet, I removed the duffle bag hidden in there. Setting the duffle on my bed, I opened it to inspect the contents of the bag. There were six kilos of coke after I took my two and rubber banded stacks of one hundred dollar bills inside.

For the next three hours, I counted and recounted the stacks of money. Once it was all accounted for, I came up with *$335,000. Damn!*

The scratching of feet against the carpet could be heard coming towards my room. Throwing the bag into the closet, I slammed it closed as my Mom barged in.

"You got my money?" she asked, with her bony hands on her skeletal hips. She was puffing on a cigarette as she looked down at me sitting on the bed.

Just to fuck with her, I replied, "nope. I need a little more time."

"I knew yo ass couldn't get no money. You aint shit like ya daddy! Pack yo shit and get the fuck out my house!" Slamming the door behind her, she left the stench of cigarette smoke lingering in my room.

Getting from the bed, I walked over to my oak dresser in the corner of my room, and opened the top drawer. I grabbed a thousand dollars out of the money La'Ron had given me and crumpled the bills into my hands. Opening the door to my room, I went into the living room to find my mom sitting on the couch.

"You're disgusting my nigga." I said tossing the money at her feet. "And you said 'nothing like my Dad? I'll laugh in your face if you really want to talk about comparisons. You aren't even close to the mother you once were. I love you though."

Without waiting on a reply, I went back into my room and slammed the door behind me. Picking up my cell phone that was on the floor next to my bed, I noticed I had a text from La'Ron.

Meet me at The Marriott in Concord, it read.

Throwing on a pair of black sweats, I grabbed the duffle bag out the closet, the keys to the Charger and was out.

Call Me, by Too Short featuring Lil Kim was bumping through the two fifteens in my trunk. It felt good to have my own set of wheels and I was eating that shit up.

Pulling up to the hotel, I grabbed the duffle bag out the backseat and went inside. La'Ron had sent me the room number and I headed straight for the elevator. When I reached level five, I got off and knocked on his door.

"Who is it?" La'Ron asked.

"It's the boogey man! Who else nigga?"

Opening the door, he had a pistol in his hands. Looking up and down the hallway as I walked pass him into the room, I took a seat on the tan sofa. I put the duffle bag on the floor at my feet as he took a seat across from me. "How you been dude?" I asked, trying to break the uncomfortable silence in the room.

"I'm straight bruh. Just trying to lay low and shit. I heard about that shit that happened last week in *The Baileys*. You good?"

"I'm straight. Wasn't nothing I couldn't handle. Business still poppin so it's whatever."

"Let me see that bag." He said, reaching his hand out. Getting it from the floor, I handed it to him as he opened it up. "Jackpot."

I watched as he pulled the six kilos of coke out of the bag. He piled them onto the table neatly before he started grabbing the money. Throwing me stack after stack, he directed me to start counting.

"I counted it this morning. It was *$335,000*. Every dollar accounted for."

After counting the money himself, he set it on the table in two piles.

"Go ahead and take that pile right there," he said, pointing to the money that sat before me. "I appreciate that stunt you pulled for me and I'll forever be indebted to you. If you hadn't of been there, I'd be six feet under."

"You serious bruh?"

"As a heart attack, that's *$170,000* dude. Make all your heart desires possible bro."

"Nigga you just giving me *$170,000* like its nothing? The fuck?" I was baffled and was trying to comprehend what the fuck was going on.

"That's a drop in the bucket for a nigga like me. Just know that I appreciate you looking out for me."

"Well shit since it seem like I'm on my way to becoming a rich nigga, let hits that strip club *Exquisite*."

"It's good everytime."

Hitting the mall was the first thing I decided to do before we hit the strip club. Shopping in San Francisco, I did major damage in every store I ran in. After a much needed wardrobe change, I was ready to bounce. I headed straight to the house to go chill before it was time to go out.

I wore in a white Gucci sweater, black Levi's, and black Foamposite sneakers.

Dialing La'Ron, I listened to the phone ring as I waited for him to answer. "Meet me at the spot. I'm going to be running a little late."

"You sure?"

"Yup."

After hanging up, I headed straight to *Exquisite*. *Hustle* by E-40 off his new **The Ball Street Journal** album was blaring through the speakers of my car. I was in the zone. When I finally pulled up to the club, I wasn't surprised to see a line outside.

After handing the keys to valet, I walked straight up to the big burly security who was working the door. Stuffing a one hundred dollar bill into the open palm of his hand, I walked through the doors as if I owned the club. Underage and carrying my gun.

Money talks, I thought.

Grabbing a seat that was low key in the back of the club, I had a perfect view of my surroundings. A thick chocolate waitress came over to my table to take my drink order. Never being the drinker nor smoker, I ordered a sprite mixed with cranberry juice and handed her a twenty dollar tip. She smiled, winked her eye, and was on her way. Dancer after dancer attempted to get a dance, but I declined.

About fifteen minutes passed until I noticed La'Ron walking into the club. Flagging him down, he took a seat next to me. Dapping each other up, he flagged another waitress down to order himself a drink.

"What can I get for you handsome?" said, the caramel complexioned waitress. She had nice boobs, a slim waist, and a phat ass.

"Hennessy, with a single ice cube." La'Ron ordered, handing her a twenty. "You ordered something?" he asked, turning to me.

"I'm straight."

We both watched as she walked away, putting an extra sway in her hips as she strutted to the bar.

Damn, I thought.

Vibing with La'Ron, it felt good to kick back and relax. Both waitresses appearing at the same time, handed over our drinks. Dimming the lights, the DJ announced the next performer.

"Now I need for all you niggas to come out of your pockets for Chocolate Paradise. She is one of the most beautiful women to ever step in the club, so all you niggas dig deep in your pockets, and quit being so cheap."

Drop it To The Clap by DJ Upgrade featuring Mob Squad played as the curtains opened. With a body like Teyana Taylor, this chocolate goddess in front of me was... stunning!

The forest green negligee she wore left nothing to the imagination as she began her set. The way she was moving her body, had me hypnotized.

My dick was hard as rock as I watched the snake like movements she made with her body. Her body was blemish free and I didn't see a stretch mark in sight. Her thick frame, slim waist, and flat stomach had me ready to bust one. Thick natural hair that she wore in loose curls.

Getting out of my seat, I made my way to the stage. *Tempo Slow* by R. Kelly mixed in. Our eyes locked as I put a twenty into the garder on her thigh.

She climbed to the top of the pole and spiraled down into a slow split. Grabbing her right leg, she flipped over and began popping her right ass cheek to the bass of one of R. Kelly's greatest.

"This look like some shit off Players Club bruh," La'Ron laughed, walking up behind me. I lusted over her body as I stayed in front of the stage. The entire time she danced, our eyes remained locked.

When she finished her set, bills of all denominations were on the stage. Picking up every single bill, she for sure made her money's worth plus extra.

Walking back to my seat, I couldn't get the mystery woman's face out of my mind.

"I'm ready to get up outta here," La'Ron said, as I took my seat on the red couch. He was slightly tipsy and although I wanted to talk to my mystery woman, I knew I needed to get this nigga out the club.

"Let's go." I said, grabbing him by one of his arms and leading him to the front door of the club. When we got outside, a misty breeze came over us. "Valet got your car?"

"Nah. I parked in the parking lot across the street."

"Come on."

Pulling away from me he said, "man I'm cool. I can make it across the street."

"Get off that bitch shit and walk across the fucking street." I said, as valet pulled my car around.

Hopping in the front seat of the Charger, I remained in the front of the club until I watched La'Ron hop in the front seat of the Range.

"Why the fuck this nigga back driving that fucking truck?" I asked aloud to myself.

Pulling off in front of me, I followed closely behind him. Rolling up to a stop sign, I lifted my phone in front of me to find a song to play through my auxiliary. A figure appearing in the back of La'Ron's truck caught my attention.

HOOOOONK!

I pressed on the horn at La'Ron to get his attention.

BOOM! BOOM!

La'Ron's back window shattered, as the shooter aimed his gun at it, targeting my head. Opening the door to my car, I rolled out onto the ground and sprang up dumping bullets at the attempted killer.

BOOM!

"Fuck!" La'Ron yelled.

I rained bullets into the car window until the nigga dropped.

Gun smoke surrounded La'Ron's car.

"I'm hit bro." He yelled out. His shoulder was hit and he was bleeding profusely.

"FUCK! FUCK!" I yelled.

"I got a lil nurse bitch that can patch me up bro. I can't go to a hospital, I'll be aiight."

"Get the fuck outta here, imma follow you!" I yelled, using the sweater I had on to push the dead body out the back of his truck.

Sirens began to sound in my ear. Running back to my Charger, I hopped in the car and peeled off behind him.

On *KTVU* channel 2 News, the shooting was being reported.

"Officials are reporting that the victim is 26 year old Ace Parks. He was executed with two bullets piercing him in the forehead and one in the neck. As of now, there have been no witnesses to come forward and it's still a developing investigation. If you have any information, please come forward."

"He's gonna be fine HaKoda, you got him here at the perfect time," Kya said, coming out the bedroom. She had been in there removing the bullet from and his shoulder and stitching him up. "I called my boss and told him I had an emergency and he's gonna prescribe me some Norco."

"Cool, gimme a minute to holla at him."

"That's fine, I'm about to go get the medicine. I already gave him a Vicodin so he's relaxing." Picking up her purse, she made her exit, locking the door behind her.

Walking into the room, I took a seat at the edge of the bed. He was lying at the head of the bed with his shoulder patched up.

"How you feelin' gangsta?"

Taking a deep breath, he responded, "they couldn't keep a real nigga down."

We both chuckled.

"I'm out the game Ko. The lifestyle is cool, the money is good, but it's not worth it. By no way am I punking out because I plan on finishing this shit before I leave the game. But in this life, you only make it out one of two ways and I'm tryna create a third before it's too late. I have more than enough money to retire from this shit and go legit."

"I feel you."

"I'm giving you the Throne bro. It's in you my nigga. In due time, you'll know when to get out."

Dapping hands, we went our separate ways. The next day I let Moms know I was moving out. She almost had a heart attack until I told her I'd still be helping her out *on one condition*. She would be going straight to rehab.

After I packed up all my shit, most importantly my money, I headed straight for Brentwood CA. La'Ron had a property that he owned that nobody knew about. I planned on making that my new residence.

Furniture, bedroom sets, television, and all the other amenities I'd need were already set up in the house.

After getting settled in, I had to go see what the streets were hollering. The first stop I made was to the barbershop, the number one gossip spot for niggas.

"What's up old man?" I greeted Ahmed, walking into the shop.

"Shit you tell me."

"I don't even know where to start."

"Meet me in the back." He said, as a multitude of niggas began entering the shop on this Saturday morning.

Now in the back, in the office, I took a seat at the desk. "Man you know the streets talking about what happened to Ace right?"

"Fuck that gotta do with me?"

"They saying La'Ron did it."

"Again, what you tryna say man?"

"Was you there when that shit happened?"

"Hell nah. He had just come by the hut to pick up some shit and then he dipped." I lied.

"I'm just glad you cool. The streets saying some young nigga by the name Donny set that shit up."

"Donny?"

"East Oakland nigga tryna take over some of the spots La'Ron was running."

Making a mental note of the information, I knew I needed to make some changes.

"I need a favor."

"Talk to me."

"I need you to hookup something with a dealer to get me a couple cars."

"What you looking for?"

"I'll let you know."

With La'Ron out, I was on my way to becoming 'That Nigga.'

Chapter Six

2014

It had been three years and I had begun to see all my dreams come to fruition. After La'Ron left *The Game*, I inherited his empire and at the age of 22, I was a Kingpin.

Going from living with my junkie Moms to a four bedroom, four bathroom mini mansion in Brentwood CA, I was living good. I still hit my Moms with money every month and life was good. She had kept up with her treatments and she was getting better.

I was on Hillcrest in Antioch when I spotted my chocolate from *Exquisite* on the side of me in a 2011 white Nissan Maxima on twenty's as she maneuvered her car in and out of traffic. Putting the pedal to the metal in my newly purchased 2015 coke white Audi A5, I followed behind her until I was on the side of her car. Pulling up to a red light, I cut off the black Buick on my right to pull up to her passenger side window.

Honking my horn at her, she rolled down her window.

"Wassup beautiful?"

I watched her blush as she answered, "nothing much. What about you?"

"I'm about to hop in traffic. Jump in front of me and turn inside Applebee's parking lot." Doing as she was told, I followed her inside the lot and parked my car. I'm sure the diamonds in my ears, my purple v-neck Gucci sweater, black Levi's, and black Gucci high top boots had her eyeing me.

Sitting behind the wheel of her car, I watched as she gave me the once over.

"May I get your name beautiful?" I asked in my smooth baritone, leaning over window.

"Akuni Iwu."

"Iwu?"

"I'm West African."

Her Hershey kissed skin, tiny black freckles, and thick natural hair that she wore in curls, slanted dark brown eyes, and with deep dimples that showed a hint of red that appeared when she blushed. Beautiful white teeth that was perfect.

"You are beautiful."

"Thank you! What's your name?"

"HaKoda."

"That's different," she said, reaching her freshly manicured hand out of the window to flip my platted dreads out my face. Now hanging to the middle of my back, I was draping.

Kissing her on the top of her hand, I said, "Can I get your number and take you out tonight if you aren't busy?"

"I'm not, and you can." She answered with a smile. After giving me her number and the address of where to pick her up from, I hopped in my Audi and sped off.

I went straight to the barbershop with *What You See* by J. Stalin bumping from my trunk. The bass was turned up and my state of the art speakers were doing their job.

Benz's, Jaguars, and Charger's were in the parking lot of the barbershop. It looked more like a car show than a place of business. When I walked inside the shop, I immediately began getting love.

"Wassup Ko?"

"What's good nigga?" I heard, dapping up a few of the dudes I knew within the establishment. It felt good to be back in the P and I felt at home as I walked up on my best friend Dammar who was in the barber chair getting cut. Sneaking up behind him, I punched him in the chest.

"Wassup nigga?" he said, getting his mustache lined up.

"I need to get my dreads lined up real quick."

"I feel it. And I see you flossing on mu'fuckas with the Gucci shit on."

Smiling, I took the compliment and had a seat in my barber's chair. Although there were people who had been there before me waiting to get cut, I sat down anyway. While I was chilling, Ahmed came from the back of the office.

"Youngin'!" he said, when he noticed me. Walking towards me, we dapped hands, and embraced for a second.

"Wassup old man?"I asked, taking in his appearance. Rocking an old school Adida sweat suit with a pair of uptowns, he looked exactly the same from when I use to work there.

"Nothing but the sun young blood. What you getting into tonight?"

"I got a date."

"Is that right? What she looking like?" he asked, taking the empty chair on my right.

"Hershey skin with a head of thick curls. Slim thick with a nice ass and one of the most beautiful faces I've ever seen man."

"You sound like you in love." He joked, before we started laughing. "But I see you youngin'."

Wrapping up our conversation, my barber Cory finally came from the back of the shop. Shaking hands, he grabbed the smock and threw it over me. "Nigga you know you not suppose to be in the chair." He said, laughing.

"It don't matter."

While getting lined up, Dammar was done getting cut. Standing over me, I took in his appearance. He had on a teal and black Kenneth Cole sweater, a pair of jeans, and some teal and black Timberlands.

"Nigga you talking about me and you got this shit on."

"You know how I do." He said, laughing. "But I got to dip so hit me later on."

"Aiight." After dapping hands one last time, he left.

Back at the house, I tried to figure out what the fuck I was about to throw on for the night. As I went through my walk in closet, the sound of my phone ringing distracted me from what I was doing.

"Speak." I answered.

"The pillows you ordered will be arriving within the week." The voice on the other end of the phone said.

"Fasho." I said before hanging up.

Pillows meaning coke in code had me smiling at the money that was about to come in. The bricks I ordered from my connect was about to make it snow in August.

After going back into my closet, I settled on a cream cardigan with a black v-neck T-shirt underneath. The black jeans I had on complimented the black Louis Vuitton boots I wore. Never being the flashy type, the only jewelry that I wore were the silver grill on the bottom row of my teeth, silver nose ring and diamonds in my ear.

I grabbed my gold iPhone 6 and sent Akuni a text letting her know I was on my way to her house. When she replied letting me know she was ready, I grabbed the keys to my matte black Plymouth Barracuda and was on my way to pick her up.

Can We Be Tight by Jagged Edge was bumping through the car. Pulling up to *Rivershore* apartments in Bay Point, I drove around until I saw her car. Sending a text, I informed her that I was outside.

Ten minutes passed before she came strutting out the house. She had on a cream crop top with black high waist jeans that hugged her body like a glove. The black oversized cardigan she wore off of her right shoulder showed the Pisces tattoo she had. A gold watch accessorized her wrist. Her hair was now parted down the middle in a wild fro of curls. Black Christian Louboutins on her feet.

As she strutted to the car with her curls bouncing, my dick jumped.

"Damn," I whispered to myself before I hopped out the car to open the passenger side door for her.

"Thanks." She said, getting into the car. Taking a peek at her ass before she slid in, a sly grin appeared on my face.

"Why you smiling?" she asked, when I got back in the car.

"Just happy to see you again beautiful." I said, still grinning.

"Boy bye, you was probably looking at my booty." She laughed.

"Guilty," I responded, cracking up.

She stood 5'6." Slim thick thighs, and a flat stomach A diamond belly piercing. C cup boobs that were sitting in that crop top. Hershey skin was glistening. Man!

I took her to *Doris and Eddies'* in the business district of San Francisco. Nice quiet atmosphere that played the slow sounds of jazz in the establishment. One of the only *upscale* black owned restaurants in The City.

"Are you guys ready to order?" asked the waiter, looking from Akuni to me.

"I'll have tilapia and brocoli, brown rice cooked in chicken broth." I ordered, handing the waiter my menu.

"And for the lady?"

"I'll have the steak well done, and lobster tails. Caesar salad and please add bacon bits."

"Anything to drink while you're waiting?"

"I'll have an apple martini, shaken, not stirred. Smith, Chante' Smith," she said, imitating Vivica A. Fox in *Two Can Play that Game*.

We both started laughing.

"I'll have water with a lot of ice, thanks."

"Water?" she asked, with her eyebrows raised.

"Yeah. I don't drink."

In the life I lived, I couldn't be anything less than on my toes. La'Ron taught me that.

"Well tell me about yourself Mr. HaKoda."

"What do you want to know?"

"Everything!"

"I'm 23 years old. I'll be 24 on the 11th,"

"That's in four days!" she interjected.

"Right," I laughed, before continuing, "I live in my own house. I own a few cars. I'm in the process of transitioning careers. I'm a Leo. I have no kids. What about you Miss Akuni Iwu?"

"I'm 24."

"Old ass," I interjected, just to be funny.

"Rude ass!" she chuckled, before continuing, "I live in my own home as well. I am a freelance photographer and promotional model."

"Wait what?! I thought you were a dancer."

She started cracking up.

"Um No, I did one amateur night at *Exquisite* as a dare from my girlfriends. Never been a stripper."

That sounded like music to my ears.

"My daddy is a Diplomat. I am an only child. I'm a Pisces, and I also have no children."

"Okay cool. Where you from?"

"Born in Sierra Leone, and moved to France during the Civil War in my country. I grew up in a boarding school with 120 other girls. Then I moved to California at 19 to go to the *Arts*

Institute of San Francisco. I graduated class of '13."

"You grew up fighting huh?" I had to ask. A girl as pretty as her had to have been going rounds everyday in a school with hella females.

"Yes I did!" she laughed. "What about you?" She asked. I caught a little hint of her French accent.

"Born and raised in San Francisco. Moved to Pittsburg with Moms, Sanaa once my Pops was murdered." I answered.

The waiter brought out our food interrupting me.

"Oh I'm sorry to hear that."

"It's cool."

"I meant to mention this to you earlier, but I really like your dreads. You have some pretty hair and the way you keep them up is really sexy. Just wanted to throw that out there," she said, sipping on her martini.

Grinning, I said, "I appreciate that gorgeous."

"Definitely."

For the remainder of the date we continued to get to know each other, and I enjoyed her company. After paying the three hundred dollar bill, we were en route to her apartment.

"Would you like to come back to my place for some champagne?" She asked.

"Sure." I answered, although I didn't drink.

I wasn't ready for the night to end, and definitely wanted to spend a little more time with her. After the hour ride, we pulled up in front of her house. Opening the car door for her, I walked behind her entering the house.

The décor of her home was set in earth tones. Light shades of brown, tans, and green. The light brown three piece couch sat atop a green plush rug. The walls were a light shade of tan. There were pictures of her and her family put up on the walls in her living room. There was a picture of her at school from years back with a beautiful mixed chick with green eyes. *Damn, they both bad.*

Walking away from the wall of photos, I took a seat on the couch. I watched her grab two champagne flutes out of her cabinet, and a bottle of champagne out of the refrigerator. Her stilettos clicked across the hardwood floor in the kitchen as she copped a squat next to me.

Popping the cork on the champagne, she poured me a glass, then herself.

"Want to hear some music?"

"Yup," I answered. I took a sip of the champagne. Getting up from the couch she strutted over to her iHome and turned her iPod on.

"This my shit." She said, as *Give Me What I Want* by Keith Sweat featuring Silk serenaded us. "You like what you see?"

Nodding my head up and down I kept my eyes glued to her. She began to remove the crop top. Still sipping on her champagne, she danced from side to side in her bra and jeans. The black La Perla bra she wore had her chest sitting right. She made her way over to me, sitting her champagne flute on the table to my left as she straddled my lap.

She was grinding on me to the beat of the song. While grinding, our lips touched and then it was on. Our kisses went from slow and sexual to animalistic as she hurriedly grabbed at my belt.

My hands roamed her body as she loosened the belt on my jeans. I got from the couch and took off my cardigan and V neck.

Standing before her in nothing but my briefs, she grabbed my hand and led me to her bedroom upstairs. Once we got inside, she pushed me to the bed. Getting on her knees, she peeled off my briefs.

Once she got an eyeful of my pipe, a grin spread across her face.

"You like what you see?" I smirked repeating her words from downstairs.

Taking the head into her mouth, she went to work on my shit. Licking from the head down the vein of my dick, my toes couldn't help but to curl at her superb head game. My hands were playing in her curls as she attempted to take my big dick down her throat. One hand was massaging my balls as she deep throated my meat.

"Damn baby," I whispered.

"Oh, you haven't felt anything yet." She said, getting from her knees.

Stepping out the jeans she wore, she seductively removed her bra and panties until she stood before me in nothing but stilettos. Getting from the bed, I pinned her down and licked from her neck to her navel.

I took my time until I reached her clit. Upon reaching it, I sucked it like my favorite piece of candy. Her hands were getting caught in my dreads trying to keep my head in place.

Moving further down, I began stabbing at her pussy with my tongue like it was a miniature dick.

"YES daddy. I LOOOOVE IT. Please don't stop," she moaned.

Taste So Good by Next was now playing. *Perfect timing.* I ate her pussy until I felt her body quiver.

"You about to cum for daddy?"

"YESSSSSS!" She let out, squeezing the purple comforter on her bed. "I'M CUMMIN!!" Her love rained down on my tongue.

She lied there panting as I walked over to my jeans for a rubber. Grabbing a magnum sized condom out of my wallet, I slid it on and proceeded to enter heaven. Her body rejected my size at first, and when I finally slid in, it was the best pussy I've had.

"You tight as fuck girl."

We were building built a slow rhythm. I rocked in and out of her and as she threw it back at me.

She attempted to switch positions but I wouldn't let her. I needed to stay in the position of control.

"This yo pussy HaKoda. OH MY GAWWWWD!"

"Of course it is."

Chapter Seven

The sounds of somebody knocking on my door awakened me out of my peaceful sleep.

The fuck? I thought grabbing my gun off my bedside table and heading towards the front door. "Who is it?" I asked, standing to the right of the right of the door, ready to shoot anything. Nobody but Dammar, knew where I rested my head, and my paranoia was at an all time high.

"I'm here delivering a package for a Mr. Cullen," said the voice on the other side of the door, using the alias I put the delivery under.

I exhaled, as I tucked the gun in my waistband. Opening the door with nothing but my sweats on,

I grabbed the clipboard the white dude held out to me and signed my alias name. Rolling in the box on a dolly, he nodded his head bye, and left the premises.

Going into my kitchen that was decorated in all black appliances, I grabbed a knife and opened the box. Cutting it open, I pulled 10 oversized couch pillows out of the box. Ripping them open, two kilos of coke were nestled neatly inside.

Cash money, I thought as I ripped open all of the pillows. Stuffing the shredded remnants of the pillows back into the box they came in, I put in the call to my loyal street lieutenants and let them know to meet me at the trap house in an hour.

Grabbing the work, I went into my room, grabbed my Louis Vuitton travel bag and stuffed them inside. Hopping in the shower and getting dressed, I was out of the house in thirty minutes.

Making my way to the trap house, I was being very cautious with the weight in the car. I made sure to do the speed limit, and obey every traffic law. When I finally pulled up to my trap house, all of my Head lieutenants were in attendance. Grabbing the bag out of my trunk, I walked into the house.

Dressed in fitted black slacks and a tailored dress shirt I was dressed the professional part. When I walked inside the house, all conversation ended.

Nodding my head to a few I passed by as I made my way to the head of the long dinner table, all eyes were on me. Putting the Louis Vuitton bag on the table, I looked around the room.

"This here gentlemen is the reason we're about to have a blizzard in the summer."

Opening the bag, I removed kilo after kilo.

Looking at every hustler in the room, I noticed the hungry look in all of their eyes. It seemed as if it was yesterday when I first approached these same men to work for me after La'Ron's departure.

"The reason that all of you are here today is because we all want the same thing. Money! You ten men are the most loyal and thoroughbred niggas around," I started, standing before the men in the same gear I had on from the night before. *"Now with La'Ron gone, I know y'all need to eat. That's where I come in. I'm ready to make some moves and I need to know whether you niggas is ready. I'm about to do what La'Ron was doing, but better!"*

I could tell I had every man's attention by the way they held on to my every word, so I continued. "La'Ron left some info with his connect and I'm already running The Baileys. I'mma eventually expand. So either you niggas is down or we enemies."

"Man fuck all dat shit you hollering! Yo bitch ass use to pick up money from us for that nigga, and now you about to be running shit? Kuz he GAVE YOU The Baileys? Get the fuck outta here, PUSSY nigga!" A dude named Blue yelled, looking at me with hate in his eyes.

A grin spread across my face as I realized I'd have to make an example out of homeboy. He sat in the chair directly across from me, mean-mugging underneath the black hoodie he wore.

Before anyone could react, a hollow point entered his brain. The silencer muffled the blast that would have drawn attention to the house. Half of his head was blown off, and everybody in the room stared at me through surprised-filled eyes.

"Now... Like I was saying before I was rudely interrupted," I resumed, tucking the gun back into the waistband of my jeans, *"if you ready to make some money, it's all good. If you not with what I'm ready to do, you know where the door is."* Nobody got up, like I knew they wouldn't. From that day forward, we were getting it.

"Wassup bro?" Dammar asked, bringing me back to reality.

"Same ole shit." I said, after removing all the coke out of the bag. "And wassup to the rest of you gentlemen?"

"Whats good bruh?" I heard simultaneously.

"Well you know its re-up time and here's the prod-" I was cut off, when my phone rang. "Excuse me."

"Speak." I answered looking at the unfamiliar number on my screen.

"Ko!" La'Ron yelled into the phone, "meet me at ya crib ASAP." He hung up and an unsettling feeling crept up my spine.

"Check this out," I said, addressing the men, "all of you niggas take two birds and make this money. Shit is being cut short and I gotta go. Handle business, and have that count correct." I said, looking each hustler in the eye.

"We got you Ko." CripCrip said, dapping my hand.

"Aiight. Meeting adjourned."

Grabbing the Louis Vuitton bag, I made a dash for my car. Pulling off the street, something told me to check my rearview mirror. I noticed an unmarked police car tailing me three cars behind.

"The fuck is going on?" I asked myself aloud, as I watched the car follow me onto the freeway. Pressing the accelerator, I was gone. Before the cop knew what was up, I hopped off the next exit, leaving the police to continue on the freeway. Grabbing my phone out of my pocket, I redialed La'Ron.

"Meet me at the *Chilis* in Concord." I hung up.

I was in my rearview every second, making sure I wasn't being tailed. Pulling into the parking lot, I hopped out of my car looking in every direction. Going inside, I let the waitress seat me as I waited impatiently for La'Ron to accompany me.

The fuck is going on and why the fuck is this nigga back? I kept asking myself.

Ten minutes passed before La'Ron pulled into the parking lot in a black Range. When he walked inside, I flagged him down and he took a seat at the table. Chocolate nigga who usually had his little fro was now sporting a shaved head with diamonds in here. My nigga had definitely changed through the years.

"Man what the hell is going on? I got you calling me on some funny shit, and the police following me. What the fuck is going on?" I was trying to keep my voice low, but I was slowly losing my cool.

"Somebody talking to them boys in blue and they're on you. From the info I received, they don't have much on you, but they're slowly building a case. You need to skip town for awhile. I got some shit set up for you in LA with my brother Geaulan."

"Fuck man!" I yelled, gaining unnecessary attention from the other patrons. "What you doing back out here bruh?"

"Settling an old beef."

"That Donny shit?"

"Yup," he replied, handing me a brand new phone.

"I put my number and Geaulan's in there. I'll get rid of that one for you." Handing him my phone, we went our separate ways.

After leaving *Chilis*, I was pulling up to Akuni's crib when I thought I was seeing shit.

"Bye Donny! I'll call you later" I heard her yell to him, before walking inside her apartment.

She didn't notice me as I pulled away from her neighborhood. *This nigga La'Ron was just talking about this Donny nigga and all of sudden, he at my bitch crib? Something aint adding up,* I thought.

I sat on the street watching Donny as he hopped into the matte black *Infiniti* truck. My trigger finger began to itch.

"He not getting away this time." I said aloud, as I followed behind him. Not trying to be noticeable, I followed him two cars behind. "He gotta go."

Following him for thirty minutes straight, he ended up on Buchanan in Pittsburg. Parking my car three houses down, I waited to make my move.

"Where you at?" Akuni asked, through the other end of the phone. I had been sitting outside of Donny's house for four hours and it was pitch black outside.

"Taking care of some business."

"When will you be done selling drugs?"

I immediately hung up the phone. *Is this bitch crazy, saying that shit over the phone?* My paranoia was at an all time high, and even though the phone was new, you could never be too safe. Turning it off, I looked up to see Donny coming out the house.

Getting out of the car, I clicked my gun off of safety and walked towards Donny. "Aye my man!" I called out to him, before he was fully into the car.

"Wassup?" He said, trying to catch a glimpse of my face in the darkness.

"My nigga told me he had something for you. Yo name Donny right?"

"Who yo nigga?"

"La'Ron."

Unable to see his facial expression, I'm sure he was shocked. I pointed my steel plated 9mm in his face. One shot was all it took to end a life, and as I squeezed the trigger, I ended La'Ron's beef permanently. Silencer still intact, I thanked the man who invented them, as I hurried back to my car. Looking in every direction to make sure I wasn't being followed, I left the scene of the crime.

As soon as I stepped foot into my home, I ran into my room to pack. While stuffing my luggage full of clothes and cash, I put in a call to my accountant.

"Mr. Fobbs," He greeted, sounding wide awake, although it was two in the morning.

"I'm on my way out of town and will be sending you a routing number to send my cash."

"That's odd, but I've learned to not ask questions. Will do sir."

"Thanks."

After hanging up, I called La'Ron.

"I was just about to call you," He said as soon as he answered the phone, "I just got off the phone with my man Geaulan. Everything is set up for your arrival."

"Cool. Let him know my plane will be arriving at ten."

"Alright," he hung up.

Lying down on my king sized bed, I thought of the snitch. I made sure to keep all my boys happy, so I couldn't see the treachery happening within.

Shit just wasn't adding up to me.

Lying low was my only option, but my trigger finger was itching to silence the rat.

Akuni blew my phone up the entire night. I couldn't shake an unsettling vibe from her and I couldn't entertain her.

Having a car service pick me up at 8:30*am*, my brain was too consumed with the snitching problem. La'Ron had a private jet waiting to take me to Los Angeles.

I arrived in LA an hour later. Pulling out my phone, I called him. "Let that man know I'm at the airport."

I sat in *Starbucks* for about fifteen minutes until a *323* number popped up on my screen.

"Who dis?"

"Geaulan. I'm outside in a gray Range Rover."

I walked out of the airport in pair of black Adidas sweats, and a custom made yellow windbreaker with white rubber duck accents. A yellow bucket-hat with duck accents covering my platted dreads. Gamma 11's on my feet.

A pair of baby blue Louboutins and the sexiest legs greeted my eyes as I approached the truck. I took in the 5'7" frame, thick thighs, c-cup boobs, butterscotch complexion, and honey blonde curls. Eyes covered in Cartier frames.

"Hello. I'm Mei'Yari," She greeted, walking over to me.

"HaKoda." I greeted back.

Damn, she bomb.

Coming around the truck, Geaulan shook my hand.

"What's good with you bro, I'm Geaulan." He was chocolate with a very low fade. He had tattoos on the left and right side of his neck.

White teeth with a slight gap that showed as he spoke.

"HaKoda."

"Nice to meet you bro." Grabbing my other bag, we loaded my shit into the truck.

"Runny told me a little about your situation and I'm happy to help you out. I was once in *The Game* and I know the risk we take when participating. But I'm a partner in some Entertainment projects so we finna be on some *Hollywood* shit."

"Runny?"

"My fault bruh, I forgot you niggas out there know him as La'Ron. But yeah, same nigga," He laughed, "Nick name. He's been my best friend since diapers bro. When he hit me up about helping you, it wasn't a second thought. He got love for you. I know about the work you've put in for e'm. It's all love over here bro."

"I appreciate that bruh."

"I'mma hook you up with a position within my company and everything will become legitimate tender."

"For sure."

When he pulled up to the mansion they lived in, I was stunned. The beautiful palace lived in made my house back in Brentwood look like a condo. It had a huge fountain in the front of the house with indigo colored water.

"This joint phat ass fuck," I complimented looking around.

"Yeah it is." Mei'Yari joked laughingly.

"Thanks." They then said, in unison.

Walking inside the castle, the décor was crazy. In the first room we passed, everything was white. The carpet was white as snow, with all white leather Italian furniture. Continuing the tour, I passed by a painting of a young boy who couldn't be older than seven.

"Y'all got kids?" I asked.

"That's my son A'Jai from a previous relationship. You got kids?"

"Nah." I replied, waving my hands.

"Check this out. I know we don't know each other and shit, but we fam bro. There is more than enough space here, so feel comfortable. At least until you can find your own space."

"Thanks for that man. I'll be out of here in no time. I just gotta hit the bank and get in touch with a realtor and I'll be good."

"I can shoot you to the bank after I show you your new place of business. And I'll hook you up with my realtor." He said.

"Good looking."

Geaulan's place of business was crazy! The huge building he operated outside of looked like somewhere Donald Trump would work. The building was tall as shit and looked like it could touch the sky.

Walking inside, I noticed the busy atmosphere. Countless movie projects graced the walls of the establishment. I was impressed. Magazine covers that I had seen everywhere from grocery stores, to newsstands. They walls were lined.

Settling in his office, I took a look around. Pictures of him and Mei'Yari with people dressed in all white graced the walls.

"You ready to make the transition from Kingpin to Businessman?" He asked, as I looked around at my new life.

"Definitely."

Chapter Eight

2015

I had been in LA for a year and everything was going smooth. Geaulan brought me into the company as a partner and I happily accepted the position. Looking over some of the investments I had put my money in to, courtesy of Geaulan, all of my dirty money was becoming legitimate tender.

From the book store I opened, to the barbershop that was almost finished being built. I had a small boutique, and the restaurant. Everything seemed to be coming together.

Chilling in my office, Geaulan came strolling in as I looked over some contracts.

"What's good?"

"Shit I can't call it. Wassup with you?" I responded.

"Nothing much. Me and the lady going to *15/30* tonight. You gone slide through?"

"Mei'Yari got a friend?"

"Nah. My lady is more of a... anti social type of female," he laughed. "Her cousins are out here for the weekend though, so try ya luck!"

Leaning back in my leather chair, I didn't answer him right away. I glanced over at the work on my desk and I knew it wasn't the best decision. "Yeah I'll go," I answered going against my better judgment. "What time?"

"*10:00pm.*"

"Alright."

Now that I had plans for this Friday night, I could no longer focus at work. After flipping through the same request forms, I left for the day.

Hopping in my 2016 white on white Jeep Wrangler with 26inch rims, I sped out of the parking lot leaving tire marks on the ground as I headed for the mall.

1Hunnid by K. Camp featuring Fetty Wap blasted out of my stereo.

> *"Aye you 1hunnid, baby*
> *I'm just tryna figure out just why that nigga hate me,*
> *I got money and I throw it with no hesitation,*
> *Sneaky bitches, they be schemin' and investigatin"*

Singing along to the lyrics, I was pumped about hitting the party. I knew I had to be fresh tonight so I knew something brand new would do the trick.

After parking my car, I entered *Hollywood & Highland* and immediately wen't store to store. I had a shoe fetish and when I spotted a pair of white suede Timberlands with silver studded tongue priced at $1200, I had to cop em.

Now that I knew what shoes I had for the night, it set the foundation for what I was wearing.

I was walking when one of the most beautiful women I've ever seen crossed my path. She was dressed as if she just stepped off the cover of *Vogue Italia*.

Her hair was bone straight with a part down the middle. She had an exotic look. She had a light brown complexion with the smoothest looking skin. My nature couldn't help but rise as I watched her ample ass bounce through her dress. Her legs were nice toned and she had piercing Asian green eyes. I watched her strut through the mall in a white jumper that fit her body like a glove. Black accessories adorned her, matching the black *Saint Laurent* purse she wore. It was something about her that I wanted to get to know. Sort of like Akuni until she got on some bullshit.

When that thought entered my mind I immediately turned around to finish my shopping without pursuing my mystery woman.

I finally found exactly what I needed and was leaving when the mystery woman appeared in front of me again. We were face to face as we attempted to get out of the same door.

"Oh excuse me," she said in the most innocent voice as I held the door open for her.

"No problem beautiful." I said as I followed behind her. She seemed to be alone as I looked around for her man or even a friend.

"You have beautiful eyes," I complimented as I took in her appearance. She definitely was a beauty.

"Thanks for the compliments," she said as I walked toward my car. I sat in my truck until she got into her car. She hopped in a black Mercedes Benz S550.

Nice car, I thought as she drove off.

Something about her had me intrigued and I planned on seeing her again. LA was only so big.

Pulling in front of my newly purchased mansion in Westwood, I hopped out my truck. Walking inside, I bypassed the black granite dining room table. I walked the left cherry wood staircase.

Inside my master bedroom sat a California King covered in black mink. Looking over at the iHome that sat on my black oak bedside table, I noticed it was only 4:00*pm*.

Closing my eyes, I let my dreams take me away.

"Hey baby." She greeted.

"Hey."

She came over and gave me a peck on the lips. Watching her take off the black Prada skirt she was wearing, I instantly got hard.

Standing before me in nothing but purple YSL pumps, she was ready.

Grabbing the universal remote off the table, I pushed the button to close the curtains in the room. Pushing another button, I turned on the voice activated music player. "Can you play Say It by Tory Lanez."

Her flat stomach was rolling as she moved her body the way I first time I encountered her. The way she danced always had a way of putting me in a trance. Our eyes were locked. When she began to twirl her hips, my mouth watered.

Getting from the bed, I removed my Armani slacks and shirt, standing before her in nothing but my briefs. With my dreads braided to the back, I lied down. Crawling onto the bed seductively, she peeled off my briefs. Licking on the head of my dick, she put her game down. My toes were curling as she licked from the head of my dick to the thick vein on the back. Once she started gargling my nuts, I wanted to blow.

"Damn baby," I moaned. My hands were intertwined in her thick curls as I guided her head up and down. Holding back so I wouldn't bust, I picked Akuni's head up. "Get on the bed."

Flipping her onto her back, I spread her legs wide open. On my hands and knees, it was time to feed. Blowing cool air on her clit, I watched her shutter.

Sticking my tongue into her wet opening, the sounds of me lapping up her wetness reverberated around the room. Her left hand was rolling her right nipple around as her right hand played in my dreads.

"Damn baby. I'm about to cum!" Sticking my thumb in her butt while nibbling on her, I felt her love raining down. Lapping up her sweet nectar, I positioned myself on top of her. Guiding my long thick dick inside her, we built a slow rhythm to the beat of the song. Going balls deep inside of her, skin smacking reverberated around the room.

When the beat to Knockin Da Boots by H-Town dropped, she started showing out.

Positioning myself behind her as she got on all fours, I entered heaven. This was her song, so I knew she was about to put on a show. She threw it back at me. Fucking to the beat of the song was something she loved to do, and at that moment, it was the best thing for the both of us. Pushing down on her back, she put her head down and arched her ass in the air. Getting up on my toes, I long stroked her.

Smacking her right ass cheek, I left an imprint. Feeling my nut building, I reached over her to play with her clit.

"Oh shit daddy. I'm about to cum again. Cum with me baby."

I nutted one of the best nuts I'd ever busted.

Then I woke up. Looking down, my dick was hard as shit with nut in my briefs.

"Damn that shit was real," I said aloud... Damn Akuni, I thought you were the one.

Hopping straight in the shower, I let the overhead waterfall cascade down my body. Washing up in *Tom Ford* Neroli Portofino shower gel, I thoroughly cleaned. After washing and rewashing my body, I stood in front of my walk-in closet in a black and gold *Versace* bath towel.

Going legit was the best thing to ever happen to me. *The Game* was never for me, and now I had everything I could need plus more.

Grabbing a pair of dark blue Armani slacks that were tailored to perfection, I threw them on the bed. An Armani baby blue fitted dress shirt accessorized with gold cuff links. Putting my gold fangs, I grabbed my sliver bottoms and fit them onto my teeth. My dreads that were always lined, were braided to the back. *Gangsta Chic.*

When the clock struck *9:30pm* I was out the door. Seated comfortably in my 2016 white on white Rolls Royce coupe, I pushed it to the club.

At 24 years old, I was doing it.

15/30 was packed. The line wrapped around the corner and when I pulled up. Looking in my rearview, Geaulan's 2016 gray Maserati Granturismo pulled up behind me.

This nigga sitting pretty, I thought when I got out of my car. I handed my keys to valet.

"Where them cousins at," I laughed, dapping hands with Geaulan.

"They're here already." Mei'Yari said, giving me a peck on the cheek as I embraced her. Over the year, Geaulan and Mei'Yari had become like a big brother and sister.

Geaulan dressed in a purple Hermes sweater and black slacks, and Mei'Yari in a black body suit and purple pencil skirt with a split up the back.

We walked into the club looking like money. Every head in the vicinity turned to stare at us. Geaulan, partnering in projects and having a name in the industry was a celebrity to these people. They showed him major love as we got further into the club. Mei'Yari was looking every thirsty broad up and down daring them to step to her nigga.

All I could do was laugh as we had a seat in VIP. Ordering a bottle of Rose' from the waitress, we all got comfortable. When Mei'Yari's cousins walked in, I drooled.

"HaKoda this is Desiree, Angel and Tanaya."

"Damn!" I said, looking all three up and down.

Desiree caramel complexioned, stood at 5'5" with loose curls in her head. Parted down the middle, she looked as if she was mixed with Asian. She wore a white tank top underneath a long black cape that hung off her shoulder, Blue high waist jeans and white platforms on her feet. A Black *Berkin* bag hanging off of her arm.

Angel brown skinned, standing at 5'6" in a black and white Zebra striped Catsuit that hugged her body and black *Louboutins*. Her hair was in a high bun with china bangs that framed her chinky eyes.

Tanaya, fair brown skin also standing at 5'6" in a black body suit and high waist olive green jeans. Her hair was dark brown with a side part. Black *Manolo Blahnik* pumps on her feet.

"Damn! All y'all gorgeous as fuck!"

They all started laughing. "Thank you!" They said in unison.

Freak Hoe by Future started blaring out the speakers and it got live. The four ladies headed to the floor and put on a show.

"This my shit!" Angel yelled, as she began putting on a show. She was popping her ass to the beat of the song.

"GOOO SIS, GO TEE!" Desiree said, cheering the both of them on.

Tanaya, pulled out her camera capturing everything as she rolled her body to the beats. Every nigga in the club was eyeing them. They were definitely *Fine China* in a building full of *Plastic Ware*.

Geaulan kept his eyes on all surrounding niggas, especially the ones eyeing Mei'Yari moving on the dance floor.

Back That Ass Up by Juvenile mixed in. We were all having a good time and it felt good to just let loose. As I was scanning the crowd, I noticed her. In a crème high waist pencil skirt and brown sweater top that crossed over her chest, was my mystery woman.

Making my way to the dance floor, I walked up behind her and began dancing. Turning around, she took in my face and danced on me.

"AYYEEEE!" The girls yelled making a crowd around us. They not once hated on the chick as we all enjoyed the atmosphere.

Once the song ended, I invited her back to VIP.

"HaKoda," I said, extending my hand to her as we got comfortable on the crush velvet seats of the club.

"Germany, pleasure to meet you… Again!" She laughed.

I took a deep stare into her Asian green eyes. She was beautiful.

"The pleasure is all mines. I wanna take you out tomorrow night. How does that sound?"

"I'm with it, gimme your number."

Putting my number in her gold iPhone 6, she remained by my side the remainder of the night and I enjoyed the company.

Chapter Nine

Two weeks had passed since I gave Germany my number and she hadn't used it. On this particular morning, I was walking through my kitchen wearing nothing but sweats. My dreads were all over the place as I opened the stainless steel refrigerator to grab a water bottle.

The Young Sam *Wrist Silly* ring tone of my phone caught my attention.

"Hello." Germany greeted, when I answered the phone.

"What's going on beautiful?"

"Not too much, how'd you sleep?"

"I slept well. Would have been better had you been here letting me hold you." I answered, taking a seat at the island in the middle of my kitchen.

"I wasn't invited," she replied.

"So I could've had a night cap had I asked?"'

"Not at all, but I would have still liked to be invited."

We both burst out laughing. "What do I owe the pleasure of this call?" I asked.

"I was thinking about you so I decided to call," she answered back.

"It's been two weeks, you weren't thinking about me," I teased.

"Yes I was, HaKODUHH!"

"Don't be saying my name like that," I laughed.

"Or what?" she flirted.

"I can show you better than I could tell you GERRRMANY!"

"Is that right?"

"Yup."

"Mhmm we'll see. So where you taking me to eat?"

I couldn't help but to laugh at the bluntness.

"What you in the mood for ma?"

"Surprise me!"

"There's a restaurant in Westwood we can go too" I suggested.

"That's fine, but I'll drive myself. I don't know you; you can't know where I live."

"I can respect it," I said with a laugh. *Independent woman*, I thought, *I like that.* "I'll text you the address."

She started laughing and we agreed to meet at *8:30pm*. After hanging up, I sat on the edge of my King sized bed and lied back. I was excited about seeing Germany again. Get to know the woman behind the *Seducing* green gaze.

I pulled up to the restaurant at exactly *8:30pm*. Being that I was busy man, tardiness was always a problem for me.

Giving the keys to my Jeep to the valet, I headed towards the entrance of the restaurant. I pulled out my phone to dial Germany. Her number popped up on my screen before I could push send.

"Yo," I answered.

"I'm running a little late and will be there in about ten minutes."

"Okay," I said as we hung up. *At least she was considerate enough to let me know she was going to be late,* I thought walking in the restaurant.

The establishment was very upscale. I had on a black cotton twill cardigan shirt with matching tailored slacks. My shirt was tucked inside my slacks, showing off the red Hermes belt I wore. A pair of black leather calf boots on my feet. A gold Movado watch adorned my wrist.

I scanned the room as I saw a few familiar faces. CEO's, Actors, and Pop Stars all frequented the place.

"Fobbs," I said to the white hostess with freckles wearing all black.

"Your room awaits Mr. Fobbs, are we expecting your guest soon?" she asked, as I took my seat in a very secluded part of the restaurant. I had garnered the attention of some of the white women in the building. I could see the lust in there eyes.

Black dick, is what their stares said to me.

Germany walked in and captivated the room. She had on a red body fitting cocktail dress with black *Jimmy Choos* on. Her hair was in a high ponytail with gold studs in her ear. She walked with the confidence and strut of a woman who knew she was the shit.

"I apologize for my tardiness. I had so much stuff going on today."

I held Germany's seat out for her to sit. I hadn't played the part of a gentleman in awhile but it was natural. I had grown accustomed to treating women like rotating toys, and was now bringing chivalry back to life.

"You are positively stunning." I said with a straight face. I couldn't help it.

"Thanks."

"That aint yo hair," I laughed, looking at it to make sure it was real. "What you mixed with?"

"My mother is Armenian and Black and my Father is Vietnamese and Black."

"I feel it. Germany, beautiful name for a beautiful lady."

"Please stop doing that," she said a little forcefully. "I appreciate the compliments but I honestly don't need them."

"My bad, my bad." I apologized with a chuckle. "Couldn't help it."

"So where did you get the name HaKoda? It's cute but different."

"Shit I don't know. My Mom name Sanaa, like *Lathan* and my Pop's name Hassan. I like my name though. It fits me."

"That name definitely fits you."

"When is your birthday?" I asked her.

"July 16th."

"Cancer?"

"Yeah, but I don't believe in signs."

"Make believe shit," I said, agreeing.

"Are you ready to order?" the waitress asked, standing before us.

"I'll have the tilapia over white rice and vegetables. Asparagus on the side, lease season it with pepper with a squeeze of fresh lemon juice. I'd like a *Gallo* red moscato if you have it. "

"And for you sir?" the waitress asked, still scribbling on her iPad.

"That sounded good. I'll have the same, substitute the wine for water."

"Sure thing sir."

"So tell me about your upbringing," Germany said. She was playing with the water in front of her.

"I'm from the Hunters Pointe projects in San Francisco. I grew up in Pittsburg, California. Pop's is gone. Relationship with Moms is somewhat strained, but I love her more than anything on this planet. What about you?"

"My full name is Germany-Skyy Nguyen. I was born and raised in San Francisco. I'm from Sunnydale. Both of my parents reside there. I have a younger sister named Brooklyn on my Dad's side. The relationship I have with my Mother is strained as well. It's been getting better though, especially after I got shot a few months back."

"Wait, what," I interjected.

"Yeah, I don't really want to talk about it." Staring deep into her green eyes, a murderous look had glazed over.

"Damn ma. Well I'm glad you good. Or else you wouldn't be here, sitting with a nigga."

She began chuckling, and the awkward moment faded.

"You read?"

"Yes! I've been very passionate about reading ever since I was a kid. Something about books just calms me, and I'm also into poetry. I graduated from the *Arts Institute of San Francisco*. You into reading?" she asked.

"My Father was big on reading and I fell in love with it as a kid. I'm big on street literature along with other genres. I've read books by *Ashley & JaQuavis, Steve Harvey, Stephen King, Donald Goines,* amongst others, but you need to check out the independent author *Bronchey Ju'Tone Sair*, 21 years old, killing it with the pen!"

"I'm going to check him out."

"Make sure you do!"

The waitress showed up with our food. The smell of the tilapia had me watering at the mouth in anticipation of diving in.

"Let's toast to the evening we're having." I said raising my glass of water to her martini glass.

"I agree." She said also raising her glass.

Clink.

"What do you do for a living?"

"I'm in the Entertainment Industry, what about you?"

"So am I," she laughed.

"Judging by that S550 you pushing, I'm sure!" I laughed.

"You seem like such a great catch. You have your own money. You're good looking, like FINE AS FUCK. You're the perfect gentleman, so what is the problem. Why are you single? You gay? AHAHAHAHAHAHAHA, no I swear I'm kidding," she laughed.

"Love is the problem," I said a little harsher than I anticipated. "My apologies didn't mean to say it like that."

"It's cool."

"I kind of like the single thing you know?"

"Understandable. Who broke your heart, if you don't mind me asking."

"The first woman to ever leave me captivated, up until I met you that is."

"She's an idiot for letting you go."

"I agree."

We shared a laugh.

"Do you have any kids?" she asked me.

"None!"

"I'm actually shocked," she revealed.

"I'm not looking to make anyone my *baby's mother*." I said, leaning into her. "When I have children, I want them to be with my *Wife*. The woman I can't sleep without. My first thought when I wake up and the last thing on my mind before I fall asleep. That's what I need."

"The first man I ever truly loved put a bullet in me." The murderous glaze took over again. "He looked me in my eyes and shot me. But the crazy thing about it is, the second nigga I put my *ALL* in too, was IN THE PROCESS OF KILLING ME!! He had hit me across the back of my head with the butt of his gun and was standing over me getting ready to shoot. My *first love* shot and killed my second, then attempted to kill me!"

A single tear slid down her face as she shed some light on her past.

"Damn ma," I said, getting from my seat taking a seat next to her. Wiping the tear out of her eyes, I planted my lips on hers. "I'm sorry them sucka ass niggas did that to you. Karma is a bitch!"

"OH! I *KNOW* it is."

The way she said it had an underlying meaning to it and she knew I caught it.

"I'd want my revenge is some shit like that happened to me too Germany, so I feel you one hunnid! All is fair when you're, *Seducing The Hustle*."

I was kissing her on her neck.

"I've already been *Seduced by The Hustle* babe."

The way she said it so hood, then started rubbing my dick through my slacks was getting me hard.

"We need that check!" I said; ready to get her to a room.

"Where we going because you still can't know where I live."

"Go to the *Beverly Wilshire*!" I said, as we stood in front of the restaurant waiting for our vehicles. I sat behind the wheel of my 2016 white on white Jeep Wrangler with 26inch rims after I opened the door and had Germany seated behind her black S550.

Boomerang by Sevyn Streeter blasted out of her speakers. "Race you there!" She peeled out and I did the same.

Ride Dick So Good by Plies blasted out of my truck.

Pushing on the accelerator, I pulled up on the side of Germany in the left lane. Rolling down the passenger side window, she started dancing.

"Got a bad lil bitch that I met in my hood
And I brag on dis bitch every chance I could
How she sit on that dick
Or How she grind on dat wood
I aint never seen a bitch Ride Dick Dis Good
She ride dick so good
She ride dick so good
Never seen a bitch Ride Dick Dis Good
She a bad lil bitch that I met in my hood
And I aint Never seen a bitch Ride Dick Dis Good"

She sang the lyrics word for word. The woman before me was stunning. The way she looked at me had me feeling her vibe.

When the light turned green, I smashed in front of her and raced her to the five star Hotel.

I opened the door for her when we finally made it there.

"What a gentleman." She acknowledged, as we walked into the lobby after giving our keys to valet.

I studied her from head to toe as our services were handled. The way she carried herself and the way she walked. Her swag was on a whole new level from the women I usually dealt with. After I paid for our room, we entered the elevator with little to no talking.

I smacked her on the ass entering the suite.

"You aint doing all that talking now are you?" I taunted, sitting on the bed.

"Yeah you saying that now."

"Come lay on the bed. Let me massage you. I got skills with these hands here," I smiled, showing off my pearly whites.

"Yeah I'm sure you do." She said, lying down on her stomach.

"You gotta come out that dress ma. I need flesh on flesh contact."

She turned and looked at me. "You hella funny," she blushed.

"I'll turn around and go get the lotion out the bathroom so you won't feel uncomfortable," I chuckled. Pulling off my shirt, I walked into the huge bathroom to get the complimentary lotion off the sink. Putting it in the microwave for *15 seconds*, I removed it and walked back into the room. She was lying face down on the bed in a black thong and her black *Jimmy Choos*.

Grabbing my phone, I hooked it up to the stereo. *Lapdance* by TeeFLii featuring Jeremih serenaded us.

Drizzling the lotion onto her back, I rubbed it in while massaging her shoulders.

I took my time with her. I needed to make her as comfortable as possible. After hearing the stories of how those niggas fucked her over, the last thing I wanted her to feel was unwanted.

I massaged her for ten minutes straight. Her face was lying on her right cheek. She let it out low moans as my hands roamed her body. Flipping over, her nipples were erect as hell

Lil mama horny.

"Let me do you now." She said licking her lips at me.

"You don't know how to use dem hands," I challenged.

"Boy bye! You're not the only one who knows how to use their hands!" Sticking my left thumb in my mouth, I cupped her left tittie and twirled her nipple.

"I guess I do have skills huh?" I smiled, staring at em.

"Shut up boy. Hand me the lotion and lay down." I did as I was told and lied on my back. I watched her scan my 6'3" frame. Her eyes told me she was ready to skip the foreplay and get straight down to business.

My entire upper half was covered in tattoos.

She was sitting directly on my dick, and felt every movement it made. Her hands roamed my body as she drizzled lotion on me. Her hands ran up and down my eight pack as she sucked on my neck. My eyes were closed enjoying the sensation.

Using my left index and middle finger, I parted her pussy lips while pulling her thong to the side with my right hand.

I kissed her lips and that was the beginning to the wild night we were about to share.

She kissed me back and it was on. I broke our kiss and started placing kisses all over her body. I traced a trail down her body with my tongue. She was riding my fingers as I played in her garden.

"I wanna feel it," she moaned, getting from off my fingers and getting on her knees. Reaching for the red *Hermes* belt I wore, she unfastened it and unbuttoned my slacks. Her hands stroked my dick through the black polo drawers I wore.

Pulling off my drawers, she licked her lips at my nine inches. *Stroke You Up* by Changing Faces began playing.

"Can I stroke you up?" I asked, referencing the song.

Without responding, she grabbed my dick and circled the head with the tip of her tongue. "You ready to be *Seduced*?" she asked.

Taking the head into her mouth, she sucked on it like her favorite lollipop. My toes curled as she took me down her throat. The head of my big ass dick was going rounds with her uvula. I felt her dry heaving on my dick.

"Lil mama can't hang." I laughed, taking my dick out of her mouth.

She blushed with embarrassment, getting from her knees. "Lemme get a rubber real quick. Safe sex is the best Sex. Aint nobody tryna receive that I'm late text."

Grabbing a magnum sized condom out of my pants, and I made my way back to the bed.

"Let me put that on you."

Getting from the bed, she took the condom out of my hand. Pushing me to sit on the edge, she repositioned herself on her knees in between my legs.

Ripping the wrapper off the condom, I watched her put it in her mouth and take me down her throat.

She trying to redeem herself, I thought.

She wrapped the condom around my dick using nothing but her mouth. *No hands!* Once it was secure, she got on top.

Putting as much of my dick that she could handle inside her, I stroked her slowly. She threw it back, and we had a good rhythm going.

"YESSSSSS!!!!!" She moaned.

I took her nipples in my mouth as she gripped my dreads. Sucking from the left to the right, we were enjoying each other.

Turning her over, I put both of her legs over my shoulders. "PUT THAT DICK BACK IN THERE!"

Doing as told, she guided my dick inside her.

"OH MY FUCKIN GAWWD HAKODAAAA!" My dick got harder as she moaned my name.

The headboard was banging on the wall. I knew the neighboring guests were getting an earful and I didn't give a *FUCK!*

"YOU FEEL ME?" I asked, stroking her. I was tickling her clit while I enjoying her wetness.

"YES BABY! I FEEL IT! UUUHHHH!!" she moaned. My dreads were all over the place as I went crazy in the pussy. Her shit felt good as a mu'fucka! "I'M ABOUT TO CUM. CUM WITH ME BABY!" She said, still throwing it at me.

"YOU WANT DADDY TO CUM BABY?"

"YESSSSS! I'M CUMMING." She started squeezing my dick with her pussy muscles and I knew she was getting ready to release. "PLEASE CUM BABE!" she moaned.

We blew at the same time.

Both of our bodies jerked as I pulled out of her and rolled onto the bed. "DAMN!" I said.

"You know you mine now!" she kissed my lips. "MINE!"

Chapter Ten

"I have a surprise for you when you get back to the room babe," Germany said through the other end of the phone. I was down the street from the hotel and couldn't wait to see what she had in store for me.

I had just come back from the office, so the first thing I did was hit the shower. We had been holed up in the room for a little under two weeks and neither was ready to budge on showing where we rested our heads permanently.

I let the steamy hot water cascade down my chiseled back as I relaxed in the shower.

I had my eyes closed when I heard a pair of stilettos *click clacking* against the floor. I knew it was Germany. When I felt the breeze on my back from the shower being open, I kept my eyes closed. I felt soft lips on my back while her hands roamed free around my body.

I was lathering my towel with soap when she grabbed it from my hands and starting washing me up. Her nails traced my back as she cleaned me.

Damn this shit feel good, I thought as her right hand landed on my dick.

Click Clack Click Clack

Am I trippin or what? I thought, unsure if I was hearing things. When the shower door opened up, I immediately turned around. Germany had just stepped into the shower. The woman in the shower with me wasn't Germany. It was a thick Latino chick with red hair.

"Since you now belong to me, I thought I'd indulge in your LAST time sampling any other pussy outside of mine. Daddy, meet Jaslene. Jaslene meet my daddy, HaKoda."

"We kind of met already," Jaslene said seductively, still massaging my dick.

"Yeah, we met," I said with a sly grin on my face. I knew today was going to be one to remember.

"Well daddy when you're done washing up, meet us in the room." Germany said, grabbing Jaslene by the hand and leading her into the room.

"Aiight."

I hurriedly washed my body thinking about the threesome that was about to pop off. After I was done washing my dick I hopped out the shower. When I walked into the room what I saw blew my mind.

Germany was sprawled across the bed with her legs gaping wide open. Jaslene was in between them, feasting. I was in heaven as I watched the freaky shit happening before me.

Jaslene was sucking on Germany's pussy like it was the last meal she'd ever taste. Germany eyes were staring directly into mine. With her head in Germany's lap, I hiked Jaslene's ass in the air. Grabbing a newly purchased condom out the bag I brought in with me, I slid it on. Sliding the head of my dick into her wetness, she moaned in pleasure.

"Fuck!" I moaned as she clenched my dick with her pussy.

"Fuck that bitch!" Germany ordered, twirling her nipples with her left hand as her right held a grip on Jaslene's head in her lap.

I was pounding Jaslene from the back while never breaking eye contact with Germany. From the moans escaping both their lips, they were loving it.

"Alright girl, you gotta move. That's MY DICK!"

Removing the condom I used on Jaslene, Germany fitted me a new one and slid it inside of her.

"RIGHT THERE!" She moaned, throwing it back at me.

These freaks had a nigga feeling like a true King. Four nuts later all of us were spent. Germany was definitely down to ride.

Chapter Eleven

I woke up the next morning to a call from a *925* area code and I immediately knew that was the Pittsburg area. I answered the phone and when I heard the voice on the other end, my knees almost buckled.

"Hey baby," said the voice I hadn't heard in years.

"Mom? Is that you?" I asked.

"Yes HaKoda. It's me. How are you sweetie?"

I hadn't heard her so full of life since before my Pops was murdered. She sounded healthy and like her old self.

"I'm good ma, doing real good things. How are you? You sound good."

"I'm good. I kept up with my rehabilitation and I am clean baby. I moved out the apartment and with you still sending me money, I enrolled in a program for first home buyers while in rehab. The money you sent me accumulated to almost half a million and I bought the house once I was fully clean. Your advisor assured me that I wouldn't have access to the funds until I was really ready to get myself together. I bought my first house yesterday and I'm doing good babe."

A small cry escaped her lips as she shared her good news with me.

I kept my emotions in check as I let her cry. I loved my Moms more than anything and I felt at peace knowing she was good.

"I'm happy to hear that Mom, I really am. How did you get my number?" I was rambling and had awoken a sleeping Germany.

"I got your number from that girl you used to run around with. The pretty chocolate one. *Lot's* of hair. You know how you like e'm. I can't think of her name right now. Erica or Ashley. Somebody! Anyway, she said she'll be seeing you soon."

"Who?" I asked, knowing none of the females from back home had my number.

Germany was now paying attention so I didn't get in too it.

"She seems to be the only person from around the way who seems to know you still exist. When I got out, she was there to pick me up."

I really couldn't figure out what the fuck she was talking about.

"Where you staying Ma? I'm coming to see you."

An eerie feeling had crept into my body and I couldn't shake it. She gave me her address and I hung up.

"Babe what's wrong and where you going?" Germany asked, as I raced around the room to grab what I'd need to take with me back to *The Bay*.

"Babe that was my Mom, something isn't sitting right with me after talking to her. I gotta head back to *The Bay*. Go to my contact list and look under the name *Retainer* and dial the second number. Tell e'm I'll be at the airport to go to Oakland in 45minutes," I said throwing her my phone.

"I got you babe. I'm going with you."

I stopped in my tracks after she finished her sentence. I wasn't willing to bring Germany into my past, especially after everything she's been through.

"I'll be back Germany. Stay here."

"I wasn't asking permission, I was informing you. We clearly have no time to go home to pack so I'll be expecting a shopping spree once we get there!" She pecked me on the lips and scrambled up her belongings.

Two hours passed and we had arrived in Oakland. There was a black Lincoln town car was waiting for us as soon as we stepped off the plane. Germany was dressed in a burgundy body suit and black high waist jean shorts. *Nunka thigh in black leather Givenchy boots* on her feet. The leather over her thigh accentuated her thick legs. Her hair was in wand curls.

In this September California weather, I was dressed in a pair of black *Dickies* shorts and a pair of white, burgundy, and tan *Nike Cortez*. Long black *Nike* socks on. A black *Burberry* T-shirt. My signature gold fangs and silver bottom grill in my mouth.

Nervous energy filled my body as we made our way to my Moms. Checking for the *.357* magnum on my waist, I had to make sure it was there. Being back in *The Bay*, I had to stay on my toes.

I didn't know how I felt about seeing her after all this time. I missed my Mom, the Mom who'd be on my line about sneaking to listen to my Dad's old drug meetings. Who'd be on me about making sure I kept my grades up. The mother who actually gave a fuck!

I knew the only reason she changed was because of the death of my Dad. But it didn't take away the pain she caused. The emptiness I had in my heart for her sometimes because of the choices she made. She was always going to be my Mother, so loving her was never going to change.

Germany squeezed my knee, assuring me she was here and wasn't going anywhere. I looked over at her and leaned in for a kiss.

I took a deep breath when we pulled up to the address my Mom had given me. She lived in *Highlands Ranch* in Pittsburg.

Germany stood right behind me as I knocked. I waited with bated breath as I waited for her to answer the door.

When the door opened and my Mother stood before looking as beautiful as I she did when I was a kid.

Tears fell out my eyes.

Her high yellow complexion was glowing. She gained some of her weight back. She had cut her hair and was wearing it in a short curly fro.

Dad would be proud.

She was crying as she embraced me. We rocked back and forth right there on the porch.

"I'm so sorry for everything I put you through HaKoda. I love you so much." She whispered into my ear repeatedly.

"I love you too." I was a little choked up.

"Hello beautiful. You're obviously the woman that has been taking care of my baby. How are you."

"I'm good. How are you?" Germany responded as my Mom broke our hug to embrace her.

Letting her go, she escorted us into the house.

"You want the driver to stay right?" Germany asked, before we fully walked inside the house.

"Yeah," I responded.
She turned back to inform the driver to sit while we sat with my Mom. I followed her to her living room and took a seat on her black and white sofa as she sat in the love seat facing me.

"HaKoda, you grew up to become the perfect blend of Hassan and I," she cried. "I missed so much of you growing up due to drugs and I need to apologize. I don't know what you had to endure while I was under the *Devils* thumb and I can only imagine how you dealt with it.

Every day that I sat in that rehabilitation center, I thought of how I treated you. How I know yo daddy would have killed me had he seen me like that, THAT'S what got me through it. I'M SORRY," she cried.

Germany walked in the living room and had a seat next to me.

"I won't sit here and lie and say I don't harbor some resentment towards you for how you treated me over the years, but I forgive you Ma. I see you really tryna get it together so I just want us to move on from here and rebuild our relationship. How we use to be."

"Me too baby." She said getting up to hug me again, "And you," she said, turning to Germany, "I really want to say thank you again. I can see the way you look at my Son that you care for him deeply. I don't know y'all situation or who you are to him exactly, but I can appreciate the concern I see in your gaze as you watch him talk. HaKoda needs all the love and care he can get, because growing up, after my Husband died, I didn't show it. so... Thank you."

"I really do care for your son Mrs. Fobbs, and you're welcome."

"I heard my son inherited traits of his Father," She laughed, trying to change the subject.

I started chuckling. Hustling became my life after she pulled that bullshit. The streets became my family. I hit the ground hard to build myself from the *The Kingpin's Son* to *The Junky's Son* to *THE KINGPIN*.

"Something like it ma, I was just *Seducing The Hustle*."

"He a good boy now tho!" Germany interjected.

We all laughed. "Claim it girl!" My Mom said, as she and Germany high fived each other.

For hours I caught my Mom up on Life, leaving out the sordid details of my past. Mom's knew *The Game* all too well, but it wasn't necessary to let her know everything. She was overly impressed with how I turned out, and it was cool talking to her. Sober.

Seeing the love she had for me shining through her hazel eyes again. Moms and Germany got to know each other and the fact that she approved of and liked her made everything so much better.

Part of the iciness in my heart had melted away now that my Mom was back in my life. I was out *The Game* and I had my Moms back. I was good.

Once it got too late, Germany and I got up to head to the hotel. Kissing my Mom on the cheek, I told her I'd be back the following morning and I loved her.

The eerie feeling had somewhat left my body although I still needed to question her about the mystery woman, but without Germany around.

She hugged Germany, and waved to us as we walked to the town car. Walking hand in hand, I noticed the driver slumped over on the driver side window.

I knew we had been in there for awhile, so I thought it'd be funny to scare him out of his sleep. I walked around the back of the car and was about to knock on the window when one of the most gruesome scenes I had ever witnessed was presented in front of me.

The driver's throat had been slit and there was a note attached to his chest with the words *'You and The Bitch got it coming -muah,'* scribbled across it with a lipstick print.

Somebody was watching me, and I immediately drew my *.357 Magnum.*

"The fuck is going on?" Germany asked, as she took in the dead driver.

"I don't know, but I know I need to get the fuck out of here, and I need to get you and my Moms outta here."

Germany reached in the black *Berkin* she wore and withdrew a pink .25 pistol.

"Where you get that gun from?" I asked, putting in a call. True, I was out of the game, but any nigga that had ever been in the game always kept ties to it.

"I always keep it on me babe, I've been shot before! You thought I wouldn't?"

She was looking around the area. She and I headed back into my Mom's house.

"Get whatever you feel is the most important shit outta here ma, you moving out *The Bay!*" I said, pacing my Moms living room.

Headlights shined through the front window of the house and I ran out the door.

"Who is that?" They asked in unison.

"Some of my peoples," I acknowledged, walking up on the black Escalade.

"Koda!" Dammar said, dapping my hand as he hopped out the truck. Goons of all ethnicities and ages hopped out of the trucks that were pulling up. Armed with assault rifles, they were ready to put in work.

"Wassup boss, it's good to know that anytime a nigga call you stay ready!"

"You know how we get down bruh. You called, we here, wassup?"

"Somebody murked my driver dude! I need you to find out who put out the hit. ASAP, like Rocky. And then imma need you to take my lady and my Moms to the Airport. They getting out of here."

"I'm already on it."

My Mom came out of her house with a suitcase packed, ready to clear the scene. The sight of all the goons in front of her house, guns drawn, and a dead body parked in front of her house was all too familiar. I tucked her in the back of the Escalade Dammar drove before kissing Germany on the lips.

"Be safe HaKoda," she said.

"I'll be fine. I'll hit you in a minute."
Dammar hopped in the driver's seat next peeled off.

For the next few hours I hit the streets, hitting every hood to see what was popping. Niggas had brought beef to my Moms spot and I intended on finding out who.

The sounds of my phone caught my attention as I drove through the *El Pueblo* projects. "What's the word bruh?" I asked as soon as I answered.

"Aint nobody beefin' wit you bruh bruh. I done put the word out and aint shit poppin. Cold Case," Dammar replied.

"Good looking."

I hung up and dialed the pilot. *Turn that ass around, I gotta get the fuck outta here and figure some shit out.*

Chapter Twelve

I arrived at the *Beverly Wilshire* hotel at 10:00*am* the next morning. Germany and my Mother were sound asleep when I entered the suite.

Germany was peacefully sleeping when I entered the room we shared. She had taken good care of my Moms while I was gone and it was time for them to see where I called home.

"Goodmorning baby," she greeted, staring out of her sleep.

"Morning babe, how'd you sleep?"

"You weren't here to sleep with me, so not too good," she said, poking her bottom lip out.

Giving her a peck on the lips, I removed the black *Burberry* shirt I had on from the previous day and walked in the room on the other side of the suite to check on my Moms. She was peacefully sleeping, and as I watched her take her breaths, I Thanked God for bringing her back.

"I want to take your Mom out babe. I want to get to know her outside of you. How does that sound?"

"If she with it, cool. I have some shit to look over for the company anyway. I think I want to produce a show."

"About?"

"*SWLA.*"

"Whatever that acronym stands for sound like it might be ratchet!" she laughed. "What will it be about?"

"I was actually thinking of having you at the center of it. I'll tell you in due time, I gotta run some shit by Geaulan. I want his wife to be a part of it as well.

"Yeah okay babe, you know I'll support you in all your endeavors."

"What time y'all leaving?"

"I don't know, I haven't even asked her yet. But when she is up, I will."

"Alright babe, I'm tired, I'm finna catch some Z's so if y'all leave before I wake up, I have a couple bands in my slacks."

"Okay."

I removed the wife beater and slacks I wore and tossed em in the corner. Climbing in the bed, I dozed off.

I awoke at 4:30*pm* to my phone buzzing. I let it go to voicemail because I was still tired. Once it rang again, I looked at my screen and it was Germany.

"Talk to me." I answered groggily.

She was sniffling and I shot up from the bed. "What's going on Germany?"

"She... she came out of nowhere. Before I could react she pulled the trigger." She cried into the phone.

"Where's my Mom Germany? Where y'all at? WHO THE FUCK IS SHE?" I yelled, pulling back on my slacks, already half way out the door.

"She shot her HaKoda, we're on our way to *Ronald Reagan UCLA Medical Center*."

I hung up the phone and ran to my car. It was as if the entire world had stopped. I ran every red light.

I pulled up to the hospital and ran to the room number Germany texted me.

My Moms was laid in the bed with her left shoulder bandaged up. That sight had my blood boiling. "What the fuck happened? Ma you okay?" she was out of it.

Germany ushering me outside, closed the door to my Mom's room. The look of murder on her face, "That bitch Akuni shot yo mama!"

Everything started coming full circle. "You know Akuni?"

"I sure the fuck do and on my Life I'm putting one in that bitch. I'm sorry about what happened to your Mother babe, and the Doctor said she'll be fine. But Akuni, I'm on her!" She declared. Looking into her green eyes, I saw a *killer*.

"What happened?"

"Your mother and I were having lunch at a little burger spot just getting to know each other. I get up to go to the bathroom and the bitch is standing behind me with a mug on her face. I'm like hey? Haven't seen you since our *Institute* days. The bitch started going off about how you left her to be with me. I already knew wassup then, so I took off on her. WE FIGHTING IN THE RESTAURANT BABE! I'm from Sunnydale, you already know once I feel the animosity, I'm throwing e'm. She was tryna pull my hair, so I dipped the bitch on the floor. This bitch grabbed the chair and threw it at me. SO YO MAMA STARTED STOMPING THE BITCH! Then she pulled a gun from her pocket and started shooting... Everyone was scattering, but... she caught her before I could reach my *.25.*"

"This shit is fucking crazy!"

"Right. But go check on your Mom babe, I need a shower and then I'll see you later. I got a COUPLE scores too settle!"

"Germany, be cool. Akuni got it coming, don't make a move without me!"

Giving me a kiss, she strutted out of the hospital with a Vengeance.

Walking back into my Mother's room, I took a seat to her left. Watching her take her breaths, I put my head in my hands and reminisced.

"Today we are all here because we've been having a problem with them Spanish mu'fuckas around the way. Now we've taken a few losses, but I want to be reassured that this shit won't happen again!"

My father Hassan overlooked the room full of men dressed all in black. "Now you Gentlemen know I'm out on bail right now, but I'll be back at trial tomorrow morning. Knowing how them Spanish niggas is, they might show up to start some shit so we got to be prepared. I paid off the janitors in the courtroom to slide some guns underneath the table for me for safety precautions."

Turning to face my Uncle Ahmed, he continued, "Ahmed, you my baby brother and I love you with all my heart. If something happens to me, I need you to make sure HaKoda and Sanaa are well taken care of."

"I got you bro," Ahmed assured him, staring deep into his eyes. At the age of thirteen, I knew a lot more than everyone thought I did. Although he tried to hide the life he lived from me, I knew my Dad ran a drug business. He would tell me he was a businessman, which wasn't a total lie since he did own clothing stores and a book store, but that isn't where all the money we had came from.

"Well now that most of the reason this meeting was called has been addressed, meeting adjourned. Oh yeah, HaKoda come here!" He wasn't looking at the door, but he knew I was listening.

I walked into the room, garnering the attention of everyone in attendance. They all nodded their heads as I made my way around the long oak table in the room. There were about twelve of my dad's most loyal soldiers in the room, but I knew there were loads more men at his service.

"What you doing listening at the door again?" he asked, grinning from ear to ear.

"I was listening so when I take over, I'll know what I have in store for me." I said seriously. The look of surprise made its way across my Dad's face, as I revealed my motives. My dad was my idol and I wanted to be exactly like him when I grew up. He stared into my hazel eyes that I inherited from my Mother and saw the seriousness of my words.

"Take over huh?" he asked. He knew I knew I was next in line to take over. He had been grooming me to take over since my thirteenth birthday this past August, and although he didn't want me in this life, he knew I'd probably end up in it anyway so he groomed me himself.

"Y'all see my Li'l man right here?" he asked, looking around the room. "He's next in line for the Empire. If something happens to me, when he turn seventeen he'll be running shit."

Everyone nodded their heads in agreement as my father continued to praise me.

"Groom e'm right Hassan, he gon' need it," Parish, a young soldier of my Dad's chimed in.

"Most definitely," my Dad acknowledged, then turned to me. Where's your mother?"

"I don't know." I answered. I had been listening since the beginning of the meeting so I had no clue.

"Okay. Well let me finish up in here, and after I'm done I'll come get you."

"Alright."

I left out the room closing the door behind me and made my way toward my room. I passed by the Picasso of myself with my parents and knew that I was blessed. I lived in a seven bedroom home in Hillsborough Heights.

"And where are you coming from?" My mom asked, as I entered the kitchen of our mansion.

I was stuck on stupid as she stood from the chair she occupied. She had her arms folded and shifted all of her weight to one side.

"From talking with Dad, Ma." I answered, walking to the stainless steel refrigerator to get a bottled water.

"Isn't your father in a meeting?" she asked, eyebrows raised.

"Yup" I replied, turning to go toward my room.

"Booyy! Didn't I tell you to keep your nosy ass from them meetings?" she asked following me into the foyer leading to the stairs.

I tried ignoring her as I took the plush carpeted stairs two at a time.

"I know you hear me!"

"Yes mom you did. But I had to talk to him."

"I don't give a f-" she was cut off at the sound of my dad calling her name.

I snickered as she waltzed back down the stairs, silk robe dragging behind her.

"I love you Mom," I said with a grin, as I walked into my room and shut the door.

Later on that night we were all seated having dinner when my father began speaking.

"Baby, I really need y'all to stay here during the trial tomorrow. I have a feeling some shit might pop off and I don't want y'all there just in case it does."

"Hassan. I love you with all my heart and when I said I do, I made a vow to be there for you through everything. I knew the risks when I *decided to be with you, and I plan on being there tomorrow. End of discussion."*

I took in my mom's high yellow complexion and couldn't do anything but smile. She was what you would call a, true ride or die.

I want my girl to be just like that when I get older, I thought as I listened to the exchange between the two.

"HaKoda!" My Mom said, pulling me out my trance.

I stood from the chair and grabbed her hand. "How you feeling?"

"I've been better!" she said, trying to crack a smile.

"I'm sorry this happened to you Ma."

Wincing in pain, she turned her head to the right, eyes closed in agony. "Ouch!"

Hitting the corner, I yelled for a nurse. Rushing into the room, they checked her out. Once everything was fine, they put her to sleep and I left.

Akuni, I got yo ass!

Chapter Thirteen

"What's good sis?" I said into the phone this afternoon.

"Wassup brother?" Mei'Yari replied cheerfully.

"Can you meet me at the office?"

"Everything okay?" She asked, concerned.

"Yeah, I just need to talk to you."

"I'll be there in twenty."

Hanging up the phone, I grabbed the keys to my 2016 white on white Rolls Royce coupe and was on my way out the door.

Akuni had a couple bullets with her name on e'm and no one was better to talk about with then the *Gangsta' Bitch* herself.

Mei'Yari pulled up in a glossy black on black 2016 Porsche Panamera with pink inserts on the rims. Wearing a one piece black Jumper and gold jewelry, Mei'Yari was always killing. Nude Louboutin pumps on her feet.

Her butterscotch complexion was glistening while her honey blonde curls framed her face. Dark brown eyes and stunning.

"I heard about what happened to your Mother, I'm sorry bro. You know what happened to my Mom, my best friend killed her. This world crazy!"

"Tell me about it. That's what I kinda wanted to talk to you about."

"Hop in" she said getting back in the car. Hopping in the passenger seat, she reversed and pulled off.

"Well imma make a long story short. A bitch I used to fuck with is the one who shot my Moms. Now, you and I've have talked and I know all the shit you've been through so that's why I came to you. I need you to find this bitch for me and I'll take it from there. You used to run shit out here after you left *Richmond*, so I know you know mu'fuckas. Her name Akuni Iwu. Can you make it happen?"

"I got you. You need anything else?"

"I need a brick."

She looked at me skeptically. "I thought you were done with *The Game*."

"I am completely done with *The Game*. I have just the perfect use for it though."

"Okay, its 14. I'll have what you need soon enough."

"Good looking out Yari."

"Always. So about this chick you running around with, when am I gonna meet her?"

"You know the premiere for season two of *Billionaire Boyz* is tonight? I'll bring her. "

"I'm with it. The car will pick you guys up by 8:00*pm.*

Taking me back to my car, I hugged her and peeled off. Dialing Germany as I headed to the hospital, I waited for her to answer.

"Wassup babe?" she answered. I could hear *Your Wish Is My Command* by Teyana Taylor bumping in her background.

"Where you going?"

Turning her music down, she took a deep breath. "HaKoda, I care for you so much, you know that right?"

"Yeah, wassup?"

"I am going to be completely honest with you because I expect the same in return. The reason my ex shot me is because I *Seduced* him into a set up and attempted to murder him." She revealed. "Somehow he survived after Herahm and I did what we did. He came back, killed him then shot me. I've been on a mission to get revenge ever since!"

"Herahm Santana, the basketball player? Hold up, I heard about that shit on the news. They kept playing a video of a fight at an engagement party on *TMZ*."

"That was me," she said.

"Damn ma, that shit crazy!" I was stunned as I weaved in and out of traffic. So, where you going with all this Germany?"

"My ex is in LA and I'm following him right now. I'm about to kill him. He's been out here low key for awhile and once I got the information I needed, I was able to find him. I have a tracker on his car and I gotta get him babe!"

"Germany, listen to me right now. Stop what you doing and meet me at the hospital. Imma take you to my house and we gone figure some shit out."

"HaKoda, I gotta do this."

"I got you Germany, just come back."

"I'll be there in a minute," she said.

After hanging up, I pulled up to the hospital. Taking the elevator up to my Mom's room, I walked into her room.

"Wassup beautiful," I greeted, kissing her on the cheek.

"Hey baby," she greeted.

"I'm taking you to my house today."

"I'll be speaking to my realtor sometime today to see what we can get for you. I know coming to LA, you didn't expect for things to go from bad in Pittsburg to worse in LA. He can find you a house anywhere you'd like."

"I'll think on it HaKoda. Where's Germany?"

"Right here!" she answered, walking through the door. Grabbing her by the waist, I kissed her as she bypassed me to give my Mom a hug.

"I like them shoes," my mom complimented, looking at the coke white Nike Huaraches she wore. The fitted black Adidas sweats and white crop top she wore was a somewhat indication of her activities. Germany was rarely dressed down and I knew she was on one. Her hair was in a fish tail braid going down her back.

"You always tryna match my fly," I said looking her up and down. I was dressed in tailored black slacks, a white dress shirt and black Giuseppe Zanotti loafers.

"Boy boom!" she said, pulling on my freshly braided dreads. "How are you feeling Miss Sanaa?" She asked, sitting on my lap as I took seat next to my Mom.

"I'm better, ready to get out of here."

"When are you're being discharged?"

"HaKoda said he taking me home today."

"We all going home," I interjected, looking at Germany.

A sly grin spread across her face.

"You budged!" she laughed, kissing me on the nose. "And that's funny because today was the day I buckled too! We going home!"

Already having everything set up, the nurse was waiting outside of the gate of my home as I pulled up. My Mom in the passenger seat of my car amd Germany was following behind.

Opening the car door for my Mom, she stepped out and looked around.

"This is beautiful!"

"Come on ma," I said, leading her inside the house. Décor was all black. From the black mink carpet in the living room, the furniture and the amenities.

"I love this HaKoda!" Germany said, looking around.

"Yall feel free to look around."

I took my Mother's belongings to the guest room on the east wing of the house. The nurse followed behind me as I showed her to their quarters. After dropping off my Mom's things, I went into my room and lied on my bed.

Germany strutted in behind me ten minutes later.

"I love your house!"

"Thank you. We going out tonight."

"Aww, my boo not tryna share me with his Mama tonight?"

"I want you to meet some family of mine,"
"Where we going?"

"The premiere of *Billionaire Boyz*, season two," I said, as she crawled under my arm.

"Okay cool. So, let's talk about what I told you earlier."

"Which part would you like to discuss?" I asked.

"How do you feel, knowing I've set up someone I loved because they fucked me over? Do you think you could ever trust me?"

She was looking me directly in the eyes.

"To keep it all the way one hunnid, the shit was shocking, but I don't put *anything* pass *anyone*. You told me during an early conversation of ours that you've been *Seduced by The Hustle*, so you gotta chalk it to *The Game*. He did You, You did Him, He did You, and now the ball is in your court. Don't miss yo *shot*!"

"I love your house HaKoda. I see you modeled your décor somewhat off what Daddy and I had in *Hillsborough Heights*." My mom said walking into my room.

"That was the inspiration for it," I said as she walked into the huge bathroom. "Did you see your room ma?"

"Yeah, I like it. I'm headed there now, my shoulder starting to hurt."

"I'll help you," Germany said, springing up to assist her.

"Thanks babe," I said, as they exited the room.

When she returned, she removed her sneakers and crawled in the bed. "I have to go home to get something to wear for tonight."

"I have a glam squad coming for you tonight. Stylist, Hair, Make-Up, all the shit."

"What time they coming?"

"About an hour, it's already almost 6:00*pm*."

"Okay, I'm gonna go chill with your Mom until they get here."

"Damn, you ditching a nigga for Moms now huh?"

"Shut up, I enjoy talking to her," she laughed, "She's very wise and beautiful. I don't know how y'all relationship was as you grew up, but she's a lovely woman."

"I know she is. It was just the circumstances. But I like that y'all bonding, go head. Wake me up once yo make up and all that shit is done."

"Babe, this is my bro and sis Geaulan and Mei'Yari. Geaulan and Mei'Yari, this my lady, Germany."

"I love your dress!" Mei'Yari complimented, as they hugged. Shaking hands with Geaulan, she took a seat in the stretch Mercedes limo.

"Thank you, I love yours too. Them shoes is killing!" Germany complimented.

Dapping hands with Geaulan, I got comfortable. "You look beautiful Yari," I complimented, looking at her in the white gown.

"You nervous baby?" I asked Germany, licking my lips at the custom made dress she wore.

"Yes, I've never been to anything like this."

"You look amazing babe, you'll be alright." The limo pulled up to the red carpet, and I guided her out as the driver opened up the door.

The paparazzi, media and fans started screaming, "Geaulan, over here! Oh MY GOSH! Is that Germany? The Germany-Skyy of the Herahm Santana scandal?"

The cameras started going crazy.

"You popping bitch! All press is good press!" Mei'Yari said, grabbing Germany and posing for the cameras. Seeing Mei'Yari comfort Germany made me smile as they showed out.

Germany and Mei'Yari walked down the red carpet turning heads. Giuliana Rancic from Fashion Police was covering for *E!News*.

"Well hello beautiful. Who are you wearing tonight?"

"I am wearing an up-and-coming designer by the name of Zaliyah Lee," Germany replied, taking a step into the glam cam so that everyone could marvel over her body in the dress. It was a black ball gown with a leather corset. Lace draping from her waist. The corset fit her like a glove.

Nicki Minaj was in attendance, draped in *Balmain*. The bitch was bad! She didn't have shit on Germany though. Natural woman, *no shade.*

"Who dat?" I overheard Drake ask, walking down the carpet.

"Don't even try it bruh, I know how you move!" I warned, thinking of how that nigga would try to have my bitch in one of his records. "Karrueche who?"

"Respect!" he laughed and tried to my dap my hand.

Once we made it inside and were seated front row, I enjoyed the show. *Billionaire Boyz* stayed true to form, and the shit was bananas.

"This is the story by Bronchey Battle correct?" Germany asked, whispering in my ear.

"Yeah," I replied, focusing on the show.

Germany and I laughed throughout the show and were enjoying each others company. I was introduced to so many stars and asked frequently was I a rapper, singer, actor, basketball player or model. It was cool to be in the light for a second.

Chapter Fourteen

The next morning I awoke to my gold iPhone 6+ ringing.

"Morning," I answered, seeing it was Mei'Yari.

"My baby brother is having a party at Exquisite Nights, you down?"

"Yeah we'll come through."

"I like Germany, she's real cool!"

"I like her too Yari, I really do."

"Treat her right HaKoda."

"All day!"

"I'll see y'all later."

We hung up and I lied back on the bed.I have that information you needed. Hanging up, Germany stared out of her sleep. "Who was that babe?"

"Yari, she invited us to an event for her brother."

"Okay cool, we just lounging around for the day?"

"Might as well."

Germany and I walked inside Exquisite Nights accompanied with Geaulan and Mei'Yari.

A butterscotch dude that favored Mei'Yari waved us over.

I saw Christina Milian and Karrueche in the building. Mei'Yari strutted in a black gown with a long split up her right thigh. Geaulan wore a yellow blazer and black slacks. He had black diamonds in his ear and his low fade looked freshly hit.

"What's good Li'l bruh?" Geaulan greeted, dapping him. "Congratulations."

"Thanks bruh," he replied.

"This is HaKoda and his lady, Germany. This is my brother Sair." He wore a white *Armani* blazer. There was a fitted black dress shirt tucked inside tailored black slacks. He stood at 6'3" with a low fade. Bruh was tatted up.

"Wassup bruh, congratulations on your success man, I'm HaKoda," I said, dapping his hands. I wore a custom made blazer. It was white with red and gold paint splats decorating it. Black tailored slacks and black loafers. A red *Hermes* belt belting the black dress shirt tucked within my slacks.

My baby was drop dead gorgeous. Standing at 5'6", she was a light brown complexion with sleek jet black hair. She had it in spiraled curls with a part down the middle. She had green Asian eyes. C-cup breast, that filled out the red *Balmain* one piece body suit she wore. Black *Jimmy Choo* stilettos were on her feet.

"Sair," he greeted, extending his hand to Germany.

"My pleasure," Germany greeted back.

"Nice to meet you, y'all get comfortable. My girl here, she somewhere in here talking to Porsha Williams,"he said, waving a waitress down.

"This is cute!" Germany yelled over the music.

"Yo girl?" Mei'Yari asked, looking surprised.

"Yeah, my girl," he replied.

"Sair, we need to talk."

"Not tonight Mei'Yari, whatever it is can wait."

I was bobbing my head to the music.

A chocolate chick accompanied with a set of light skin twins made their way towards us in VIP. The chocolate one wore a white top that accentuated her ample breast. A silk knee length white skirt that crossed over her thick hips. Gold *Christian Louboutins* that strapped around her ankle were on her feet. Gold studs in her ear.

One twin wore a black thigh length *Yeezus* T-shirt with knee high leather *Tom Ford* boots. She completed it with a long leather coat.

Her sister wore a green turtle neck and leather circle skirt with pleats. A gold chunky bracelet on her left wrist and a leather bomber jacket draped her shoulders. Nude *Christian Louboutin* stilettos were on her feet.

"Germany and HaKoda, this is my lady -"

"JYON!" Mei'Yari yelled, cutting Sair off before he could introduce his girl.

"I'm sorry have we met?" Jyon asked, looking at Mei'Yari dumbfounded.

"BITCH YOU KNOW WHO THE FUCK I AM!"

"I am confused as fuck. Who is this Sair?" She said.

I was peeping everything as the exchange happened.

"This is my sister Mei'Yari," he replied, stepping in front of Mei'Yari, "what's going on bruh?"

"Yeah, what's the problem?" Jyon asked.

Mei'Yari rushed pass him and punched Jyon square in the mouth.

"BITCH!" Mei'Yari grabbed a fist full of Jyon's hair with her right hand and slammed her left fist into her face repeatedly.

The twin wearing the *Yeezus* shirt stuck Mei'Yari with a left jab to the cheek. Germany, who was still seated on the velvet couch, kicked her in the stomach.

She toppled to the ground. Germany jumped on her and it was over. She rained punches to her face.

Her twin ran over to jump in.

"Bitch I wish you would touch her!" I
warned, stepping in front of her.

Germany was wearing the twin out.

BOOP!

BOOP!

Geaulan was pulling at Mei'Yari trying to get her
off Jyon. "Stop Mei'Yari! Get up!"

"STAY" **BOOP!**

"THE" **BOOP!**

"FUCK" **BOOP!**

"AWAY" **BOOP! BOOP!**

"FROM" **BOOP!**

"MY BROTHER BITCH" Mei'Yari yelled,
fighting Geaulan to get to Jyon. "I'll kill you!"

I grabbed wrestled Germany off the twin. She was
fighting to get back to her. "Relax ma," I
whispered in her ear as I dragged her toward the
exit. Next thing I felt was a bottle across my face.
A light skin dude with curly hair and blue eyes had
snuck me with a champagne bottle.

POP!

I stumbled over and Germany stole on dude. Sair sprinted in our direction and took off on dude.

BOOP! BOOP!

He two pieced him, coming out his blazer off. "What's good fuck nigga?" Sair yelled.

The cameras were catching everything.

I rushed dude and went to work.

BOOP! BOOP!

He fell over and I started stomping him. Germany and the twin had locked up again. I stomped him repeatedly.

All hell had broken loose in the club as everyone pushed to exit the establishment.

Fight after fight broke out. I looked over my shoulder to see Mei'Yari, barefoot racing back into the club.

The other twin was pulling Germany by her hair hitting her. Germany held twin, upper cutting her repeatedly in the face.

The bitch was leaking.

Mei'Yari sprang on the other twin.

BAM! BAM! BOOP!

"Let's go babe!" I yelled, grabbing Germany.

"LET GO OF ME SAIR!" Mei'Yari yelled, fighting her brother as he grabbed her off the twin.

"GRAB HER BRUH!" Sair yelled to Geaulan.

The sounds of gun shots erupted in the club and we sprinted out the door. Red and blue lights flashed outside as we ran to the car. We hopped in the Rolls Royce coupe and sped off. Sair was following behind me in a grey 2016 Bentley Muslanne.

The screeching tires of Mei'Yari's 2016 black Porsche Panamera peeled away from the club.

"This shit crazy," Germany laughed, looking in the mirror. She had a little blood spewing from the right corner of her mouth.

"I didn't expect the night to go like this," I chuckled, finding humor in the situation.

Mei'Yari called my phone as I followed behind her. "You good?"

"I'm fine, I'm sorry the night turned out like this. Tell Germany I'm sorry!"

Germany grabbed the phone and put it to her ear, "girl bye, aint nothing to apologize for. I'm sure you had your reasons. You good?"

"I'm straight," Mei'Yari answered as Germany put her on speaker.

"What was that shit about?" I asked.

"I killed her brother. We used to date, he put his hands on me. I shot him then blew his house up. Too much been going on and I think she has something to do with it."

"And that's your brother's chick? How that happen?"

"It's a long story, and he wont even answer my call for me to explain."

"Y'all gone make it work. I gotta thank bruh for having me when dude snuck me."

"I'll shoot you his number. Thanks again and I'll make up for this, I promise!"

"It's good Yari, hit me tomorrow."

We hung up and I headed home laughing at the events of the night.

"That bitch Mei'Yari crazy as fuck. I LOVE IT!" Germany laughed.

"Yeah she is."

Chapter Fifteen

I awoke to a phone call from Mei'Yari the next morning. "What's good?" I answered groggily.

"I have something that shall make you feel better about what happened last night."

"You must have what I need?"

"Yup, so I'll see you in a minute.

"Fasho, see you in a minute."

Hanging up, Germany stared out of her sleep. "Who was that babe?"

"Yari, she got some shit for us,"

"Concerning?"

"Akuni."

She sprang out of the bed. "Great, because I'm ready to get this shit over with!"

Stepping into the black *Jimmy Choo* stilettos she wore the previous night, I couldn't help but laugh.

"Why you put them shoes on?" I asked, scanning her from head to toe.

Standing before me in a black silk negligee and heels, she looked more like she was trying to give a show then plot on a bitch.

"I'm just a fly bitch! But I'll cover up," she said, laughingly, grabbing a long silk robe and belting it.

"Better? It kinda looks like a dress now," she said, prancing over to give me a kiss. Smacking her on the ass, she led me down the stairs.

"Your mother said she wants to move to Atlanta," she whispered in my ear just as the intercom buzzed, announcing Mei'Yari's arrival. Pushing a button on the wall, I let her in.

Walking into my dining room, Germany met Mei'Yari at the door to let her in. I had a seat on the couch.

Leather overalls and black *Chanel* pumps on, Mei'Yari took a seat at the table and dropped the gray *Jessica Simpson* tote bag she carried on the table.

Reaching for the purse, I opened it. Delicately wrapped in saran wrap, I removed the brick of cocaine.

"Babe run up stairs and go in my drawer and grabbed that envelope for Yari please."

"Do even worry about it, just because of last night. I have something else for you in the bag."

Reaching inside, I removed a manila folder. There was a photo of Akuni entering a salon, her address, a spare key to the BMW she was driving and a tracking device. "How the fuck you get a key to her car my nigga?" I laughed.

"I know people," she cheesed. Looking at Germany, she said "after my friend shot Geaulan, I lost it! When I look in your eyes, I see a little bit of myself. I know you're going with him to handle this bitch, so when you're done, we need to hang out! I like you, and I hate bitches! We need to get acquainted."

"I like you too, and you already know what time it is! But after it's handled, we're definitely on!"

That reminded me, "Yari!" I said, as she headed for the front door, "I'm in the process of developing a reality show. I want to revolve it around the two of you, would you consider?"

She took a long look at me before responding, "I'll think on it, and give Germany my number please. Be safe HaKoda!"

She exited the house and Germany followed behind me up the stairs carrying the tote.

"I'm ready to get it poppin," Germany announced, racing into the shower. Stuffing the brick back into the tote, I removed the wife beater and sweats I wore and accompanied her.

"Hurry up babe, we aint got time for all this lovey dovey shit, I WANT THIS BITCH!" Germany said, hurriedly washing her body.

We lathered up quick and got dressed in little to no talking. Black Adidas *women's* shorts, and a black Adidas sports bra on. Germany tied her hair in a bun and laced her size six suede gray Timberlands. *City bitch forreal,* I thought.

Gray Adidas sweats and cool grey 9 Air Jordan's on my feet. I wore a white V-neck that displayed my tattoos. My dreads were braided to the back.

Exiting the house, I turned on the tracking device to get a location on Akuni. "She at that Hair Salon in Compton," I said, getting her exact location.

We hopped in Germany's S550 and headed there.

We pulled up to the Salon off *Rosecrans Ave* in Compton thirty minutes later and parked across the street.

"You know what to do," I said, giving Germany the key to Akuni's silver BMW 645.

Hopping out the car, Germany raced across the street with the tote bag in tow. Unlocking Akuni's

BMW, she put the coke in her car. Setting the bag on the floor, she returned carrying a purse that looked exactly the same.

"Mei'Yari be on her shit!" Germany said, thinking along the same lines as me.

Mei'Yari had a replica of the purse Akuni was wearing today when the photo was taken. Swap the purses, she has the coke, instant *Karma*. We sat waiting across the street from the salon until she emerged.

"I want to fight her!" Germany said, hitting the steering wheel.

"Nah babe, she gone get hers."

"Fuck that!" Germany yelled, letting her emotions get the best of her. She slammed open her car door and sprinted across the street.

I exited the car just as Germany grabbed a handful of Akuni's thick hair and slammed her head in to the BMW.

"You thought it was good?" Germany asked, holding Akuni's head down repeatedly, upper cutting her.

"You weak ass bitch, square the fuck up!" Akuni yelled, blood gushing from her nose.

Letting her go, Germany was pumped. "C'mon bitch!"

Akuni dropped her bag and rushed Germany. Side stepping her, Germany jabbed her in the right cheek.

"Bitch I want yo motha' fuckin HEAD!" Germany said, slamming her right fist into her left hand every word she spoke.

A crowd had formed in the Compton neighborhood and it was a full on *show*. The girls locked up and it was on. Akuni, dressed in jean shorts and Jordan's had the look of hate in her eyes.

Akuni, pulling Germany's hair, yanked her down by her bun. Giving her an upper cut to her cheek, Germany rushed her forward until she fell over the curb.

"BITCH! FUCK YOU!" Germany rained punched after punch to Akuni's face.

"Get up babe, it's over with." I said, lifting Germany off Akuni.

Swinging her gray suede Timberland, Germany connected with Akuni's mouth as she got from the ground.

Sirens sounded in the distance, so we sprinted across the street to the Benz. Akuni's BMW raced down the street as we hit a U-Turn in the street and followed.

Grabbing her phone, Germany dialed *911*.

"NINE ONE ONE, what's your emergency?" asked the dispatcher.

"There is a crazy driver in front of me swerving in and out of traffic. I'm afraid she's going to hurt someone and I need the Police to get her off the road. Her license plate is N A T U R A L. It's a silver BMW 645, in Compton.

Click.

"You crazy babe," I laughed.

"That bitch finna do some time. She had to catch it before she goes in!"

A patrol car pulled up behind Akuni. She was on the phone going off from what I could see. Pulling her over in the parking lot of McDonald's, we parked to watch the scene unfold. The officer walked over to her and I'm guessing asked for her license and registration. Then all hell broke loose! His gun was drawn as he pulled her from the car.

"I put my .25 in the purse too," Germany laughed!

Akuni was in handcuffs as he radioed in for back up. Sirens could be heard getting closer to the area.

"Time to get the fuck out of here." I said, as we drove away, leaving Akuni with close to twenty years lingering over her head. Payback is a bitch.

Pulling out my iPhone, I dialed Geaulan as we headed to the house.

"I was just calling you. Guess who out here bruh? La'Ron."

"Oh word? Bring that nigga to the house."

"Aiight, we'll be there in a minute."

I hung up and took a deep sigh.

"Who was that babe?"

"Geaulan. My boy La'Ron out here, I guess. They gone meet us at the house."

"La'Ron?" she quizzed.

"Yeah, him and Geaulan could damn near be brothers. Dark niggas, but La'Ron shaved his head bald and shit."

"You know I love you HaKoda. I've been through a lot, but the connection you and I have is unlike any I've felt. I'd do anything for you. I'm loyal and would never hurt you, you know that right?"

"Yeah, I love you too ma," I said sincerely. Germany was everything I wanted in a woman since I used to watch the relationship between my Mom and Pops.

"You trust me?" She asked.

"Yeah."

"You got your gun on you?"

"Always," replied, unsure of where she was going with this.

"Can I hold it?"

The thought of her setting up her nigga previously popped into my brain. We sat in silence up until we pulled into the house. Grabbing my strap out of my waistband, I handed it to her and we walked into the house.

"Let them in when they buzz babe," I said, racing up the stairs. Running into my bedroom, I went underneath my bathroom sink and grabbed the .380 semiautomatic pistol. The intercom signaled, letting me know they had arrived.

"Germany?" I said, walking down the stairs.

"I'm in the bathroom!" she called.

Pushing the button on the wall, I buzzed them in. Unlocking the door, I opened it to greet my bros. "Whats good bro?" I greeted Geaulan. Bypassing me, he made his way inside as La'Ron came over to dap my hand and show love.

"Whats poppin baby Shiny head ass nigga," I joked, taking my bro in.

Chocolate nigga, diamonds in his ear, bald head dressed in a black tank top shirt and black Jeans.

"Niggas got jokes," he laughed.

"Come in bro," I said, leading him inside.

"Babe, come meet my bro La'Ron," I called.

Germany walked around the corner pointing her gun at La'Ron.

"Surprised?" she asked, the look of death on her face.

"What the fuck is you doing?" I asked, slowly removing the gun from my pocket.

"HaKoda, the ex that I've been tracking, the one who shot me and left me for dead is your *BRO*. La'Ron Sincere Combs."

BOOM!

Catch up with Germany in the first installment of the *Seduced* series.

Seduced
by
The Hustle

Bronchey JuTone Sair

Epilogue

We sat inside Herahm's white 2016 Ferrari Laferrari in front of the park with Ty Dolla Sign's Paranoid playing softly in the background. The song was definitely befitting for the occasion, since the last time I was in the presence of him, we were not on the best of terms. My instincts were at an all-time high and something about this situation didn't feel right to me. My instincts had never steered me wrong before, and I just couldn't shake the nerves.

"Germany!" He said, pulling me out of my thoughts.

"Wassup Herahm? What is it exactly that you need to say to me?" I asked.

"I have you out here to see if we could possibly fix what was broken in our relationship."

"Herahm, you have to be fucking kidding me! You cheated on me and got a bitch pregnant! You really think I want yo dirty dick ass after some shit like that? Get the fuck outta here." I rolled my eyes at his black ass and turned my head.

"Look Germany, I don't know how many times I have to apologize to make this right, but I can't or won't live without you."

There was a underlying message in what he just said, and I felt it.

"You don't have a choice, because I'm all the way done. You don't even realize how much I loved you. Would have done anything for you! I worshipped the ground you walked on. When you were happy, I was happy. When you were hurting, so was I. Your smile made me melt. The way you held me made me weak. The way you touched me drove me crazy. But the moment you started sharing yourself with every other bitch, you became less special."

Tears began falling at this point, but I finally had the chance to tell him how much he hurt me and I couldn't stop.

"I don't want you anymore Herahm," I finished, wiping the tears from my eyes. "I asked you that day we were in the bed when I woke up in the middle of the night to not hurt me. And this is the shit you do!"

"Germany, I'm sorry, please believe me. Do you remember the first time we met? It was two years ago in the same park we're in right now. Why you think I brought you here? I want to fix this."

"NO! What the fuck did I just tell you. There is nothing to fucking fix! It's over, so shut the fuck up talking to me! I gotta get the fuck outta here," I yelled. All the hatred I had for him began bubbling to the surface, and I needed this nigga out of my presence.

"Germany-Skyy Santana!" He started, adding fuel to the fire.

"If you don't shut the fuck up, I'm getting the fuck out."

"You better stop cutting me off while I'm fucking talking!" He warned, before continuing, "like I was about to say, I won't live without you

Germany. You belong to me!" A crazy look glazed over his eyes and it was unsettling.

"Fuck it, I'm gone." I spat in his face and flung my door open.

"Germany!" he yelled, hopping out of the car behind me.

I continued walking and never turned around to see whether he was following behind me or not. The sounds of my Jimmy Choos click clacking on the pavement beneath me sounded off in the deserted lot. By time I finally turned around, it was too late.

BAM! He hit me on the side of my head with the butt of his gun. I went crashing straight to the ground.

Oh my god, he's going to kill me, was the first thought that crossed my mind.

"Bitch I tried to keep it simple with yo mu'fucking ass, but you just don't know how to act. I told you I wouldn't live without you and I meant that shit." He stood above me with his silver plated pistol pointing directly at my mouth.

"I'mma pop you right in yo fucking grill since yo mouth so fucking greasy."

Before I could even beg for my life the next thing I heard was the blast of a gun.

Chapter One

Two Years Earlier

"I just a need a hundred to be able to pay my rent," I begged my mom as we sat at the local *Applebees*.

"What's going on with your hours at that stupid store you're working at?" She quizzed.

"*Forever 21* aint giving up no hours ma."

"My poor Germany, if you only knew how to use your assets to your advantage. You wouldn't be stuck in this position," she huffed, pulling the money out of her purse.

"Not this again ma, I know what I look like, but that doesn't mean I need to use my looks to get ahead. I will make my own way in this world without asking a man for anything. **THAT**, will only get you so far... *You should know*," I said, whispering the last part under my breath.

"Okay smart ass, you say all of that but you sitting here asking me for money."

I rolled my eyes as I looked from the burnt orange colored *Hermes* bag she was rocking, to the diamond studs she had in her ears. Armenian and Black, my mother was absolutely stunning. Light brown complexion with emerald green eyes and a head full of sleek jet black hair, Moms never had trouble with the fellas.

"I saw you roll your eyes at me young lady. All I'm saying is; you are beautiful Germany. Even more beautiful than me, and you know mama a bad bitch!" We both started laughing before she continued, "but seriously babe, you are. Once you start to believe it, the world is yours. You have that beautiful light brown complexion with those beautiful eyes we both inherited from your grandmother. All that hair, and to add, you are mixed with Vietnamese. Your eyes are colored and slanted. Girl bye! Once you get rid of them glasses and those loose ass clothes you wear, it's on."

"I hear you ma, I really do." I said, hoping she'd just shut up. We had this same conversation so often, I knew it by heart. Truth is, I knew I was beautiful. I didn't look like any of the other girls from around the way and I was told that often. But growing up with a mother who had a different male companion every other week, beauty was something I tended to run from. I didn't want to be that female that changed my man like I changed my underwear. When I was ready to unleash the beast that lay dormant underneath the glasses and sweaters I wore, it'd be for the right reasons.

Our lunch continued as usual until we went our separate ways.

Back at home in my one bedroom apartment, I ran through my homework, while periodically checking the time. It was the night of the annual charity basketball game in Oakland and I knew I needed to be there. Being a full-time student at the *Arts Institute of San Francisco*, while also working a dead-end job, I never had time to get out. I was getting ready to graduate, and another step towards getting my shit together. But tonight, I had to make an exception.

7:00pm rolled around a lot faster than I anticipated. I had just finished my sketches for my fashion design class when my phone rang.

"Hey girl," I answered, putting my earphones in my ear as I walked into my bedroom.

"You getting ready?" My sister Brooklyn asked from the other end of the phone.

"I just finished getting my homework done, so now I'm in this closet tryna find something to throw on."

"Well I'm half way done getting ready so most likely I'll probably end up meeting you up there."

"That's fine, it wont take me long."

"You talked to daddy?"

That caught me completely off guard. "No, where that come from?"

"He called me today tryna play daddy," she laughed. "Trying to question me about what I been up too, and what I should be doing. On some blah blah shit."

"Nah, bruh know not to hit my phone with that bullshit. I done had enough of one parent for the day so I refuse to hear shit from his absent ass. Nigga should have been hollering about some coins, the fuck!" We burst out cracking up.

"Right, but get dress because I should be leaving in about twenty minutes."

"Okay."

We hung up and I raced to the shower. Lathering my towel with body wash, I thoroughly cleaned myself while thinking about what I'd throw on once I got out. Mentally traveling through my closet, I knew I wanted to be comfortable but my Moms words also kept playing in my head.

Getting out the shower, I stood in my closet in just my towel. I kept avoiding the floor-length mirror that was built into the closet to stop myself from staring at my reflection. I tried to avoid it until I couldn't anymore. I dropped the towel from my body and stood there naked.

Standing at 5'6", light brown complexion with sleek jet black hair that hung to the middle of my back, you'd have to be blind to mistake my beauty. C-cup breast, flat as a board stomach with a set of thick thighs and an ass that Stevie Wonder couldn't miss, I was a dime.

"You gone be something so vicious when you get older." The voice kept repeating in my head.

I removed my glasses from my eyes and stared into them deeply. A single tear slid down and my face and turned from my reflection.

I threw on a pair of black sweats, a hoodie and some Timbs. My hair was in a high bun. I put on my white-gold bottom grill and headed out the door.

Inside of my burgundy 2008 Toyota Avalon, I turned the key over to hear no engine start. "You gotta be fucking kidding me!" I turned the key over once more to get the same result. "What the fuck!"

Grabbing my iPhone out of my purse, I hurriedly dialed Brooklyn. Please pick up, I whispered just as she answered the phone. "Please tell me you haven't left yet!"

"I'm walking out the door now. What's wrong?"

"Bitch my fucking car won't start! Come get me."

"You lucky we live a block from each other," she laughed before we hung up.

Five minutes later I was seated cozily in her 2004 Honda Accord headed to East Oakland.

"What the fuck are you wearing Germany?"

"Some sweats?"

"Exactly. You out here dressed like a bum knowing it's gone be hella niggas out here."

"Girl bye." I rolled my eyes.

She had *Shake that Monkey* by Too Short blasting out of the two 10's in her trunk. Her long hombre colored hair was parted down the middle and was swinging from side to side as she bounced in her seat. Brooklyn was ten months younger than me and I loved my sister to death. Her yellow complexion, asian eyes, and slim thick frame, my sis was bomb. We met when I was 10, after not even knowing each other existed, but once we did, we were inseparable.

"Turn that up, you know that's my song." She turned it up and we turned up all the way to the game.

We turned heads as soon as we stepped into the building. Brooklyn, standing at 5'4", had on a pair of denim overalls that she left hanging in the front. A white long-sleeve half shirt and a pair of wheat colored timbs. We luckily came across two open seats in the front row and immediately snagged em.

The Jaguars, which was the home team was trailing behind by three points. Guy after guy stepped to us as we attempted to watch the game. A light skin dude had caught Brooklyn's eye, because next thing I knew, I was sitting by myself as she moved to the other end of the court to chop it up with him.

I sat watching the game for awhile until a dark-skinned cutie with gray eyes copped a squat next to me.

"Wassup gorgeous," he greeted, turning his body to face me.

"Hello," I greeted, while discreetly looking him up and down. His right arm was covered in tattoos, and he had silver bottoms in his mouth. His hair was cut in a clean fade, and he had some of the prettiest hair I'd ever seen on a dark-skin nigga. He wore all black with a pair of pony leopard Louboutins on his feet.

"May I get your name?" His gray eyes were hypnotizing.

"Germany, and yourself?"

"I'm Herahm, my pleasure to make your acquaintance. And I'm sure you get this often, but your eyes are beautiful."

I started blushing before replying, "thank you. It's funny because I was just thinking the same thing about yours."

"Thanks beautiful. I'm not trying to get too personal… yet, but why you sitting out here alone? I know ya man's must've wandered off somewhere for a minute because I know you not out here by yourself."

"Yet?" I laughed. "That was cute how you just tried to slide that up in there. But I'm here with my sister," I replied, pointing in Brooklyn's direction.

"Oh okay, she over there chopping it with my young nigga Maurice."

"I guess," I replied, turning back to the game. I noticed some of the females had begun giving me salty looks, and I could only imagine it had something to do with the slick talking nigga seated next to me.

"Did I do something wrong?" He asked.

"Not at all, just noticed some of your fans been giving me the evil eye so I'm just watching my surroundings."

"A woman who doesn't let her guard down in the presence of the unknown? I like that."

"I'm sure." He kept tryna make small talk but something about these females was just throwing me off. I caught them ice grilling me then turning their attention to Brooklyn. But once them three big burly bitches started making their way towards Brooklyn, I already knew what time it was.

"Excuse me," I said, getting from my seat as I followed behind those three bitches who were walking up on my sister.

"Wassup bitch!" I heard the leader of the three yell to Brooklyn. Brooklyn without a second thought punched that bitch in her face and it was on. I snatched up both of the bitches who were with the other one and tagged that ass.

Growing up in Sunnydale, bitches use to pick with me often because I was pretty. But this pretty bitch can run with the best of em. I two pieced the big bitch with the singles in her head and then squared up with the other one.

"Bitch yo weak ass gone sneak up from behind!" Yelled the one wearing the baby phat outfit.

"So wassup?" I said, right before I clocked her in her nose. Blood gushed out like a leaking faucet. I followed that with two jabs before that bitch dropped.

I ran over to where Brooklyn and the other bitch was chunking em and kicked that bitch in her back. "You got my sister fucked up bitch!" I yelled, grabbing that hoe by her weave. I rammed my fist into that bitch face repeatedly until the bitch with the braids came and pulled me by my bun. She snuck me with a good one to the cheek, I recovered and rushed that bitch to the ground. I was on top of her raining haymakers to her face.

Bitches like this always seemed to take me out of my element. I kept punching her until I felt somebody pulling me off of her. I was ready to swing again when I realized it was Herahm.

"Relax lil mama, you got em."

"Fuck all of that, where the fuck is my sister?" By this time it was complete chaos going on, and I knew all too well how this shit was about to end. We was deep in the East, and them niggas shoot guns like it was a sport.

"She right here," he said, pointing to Brooklyn who was headed to the car with Maurice in tow.

"I gotta go!"

I ran to the car behind Brooklyn just as the bullets started flying. "Drive bitch!" I yelled as we peeled out of there.

"Who the fuck was those bitches?" She asked, as we hopped on the freeway headed back to San Francisco.

"I have no idea, but they got what they was looking for."

"Girl yo ass was fighting two at once!" She laughed.

"I mean, shit we had to divide em and you was already fighting that big bitch so I took off!"

"Thanks for having my back sis."

"I always will!"

Gangsta' Bitch

The Mei'Yari Lewis story

Bronchey Ju'Tone Sair

Chapter One

Hood Shit

Richmond, CA

I could hear screaming coming from the inside of my apartment as I walked up the concrete stairs. I shook my head at the ghetto-ness of the situation as I put my keys in the door to let myself inside. My mother was lying on the kitchen floor bleeding from the huge gash on her forehead. My dad was standing on top of her with a skillet in his hands.

"Bitch didn't I tell you to have my fucking dinner ready by time I got home? It's four fucking o'clock and you just now getting ready to start cooking this shit!"

"Mike you told me you'd be home by six. I thought I had enough time to have your dinner ready by time you got here. I promise it won't happen again!" My Mom pleaded.

"I'm sick of these fucking excuses Diane. You always got some excuse as to why the shit not done. I'm tired of this shit!" My dad had a deranged look in his face and I was frozen in place as he started kicking my mom in the abdomen. My Mom was seven months pregnant with my baby brother and to see him treat her that way had me ready to go postal.

"Daddy stop! I'm so fucking sick and tired of you coming in here putting your hands on us. How about you just take yo drunk ass somewhere else and leave us the fuck alone!" My dad was an alcoholic upset with his own life. One dead end job after another was the root of all his problems. I was up to my last straw with this bullshit. I had seen my Mom receive more ass whoopings and black eyes then any indication of love that I could remember. There weren't any peaceful moments in the Lewis household and if shit didn't change quick, I knew somebody was going to end up dead.

"Bitch what the fuck yo lil fast ass say to me?" My Mom's eyes looked from him to me as he turned his rage to me.

"No Mei'Yari, it's okay. Just go in your room and everything will be ok."

"No Mom, fuck that! This sorry excuse for a man needs to get the fuck up outta here. I'm tired of this shit!"

"Oh you think you grown now huh? Done started having sex and you think you can say anything you want to me huh?" He was looking at me with a perverted look in his eye and it was very unsettling. "Well imma show you just how grown you really are!" This nigga started pulling at my shirt like he was about to rape me.

Fear paralyzed me as he started pulling me to the ground. It took about a second after he pulled my blouse off of me leaving me standing in the living room in my black lace bra for me to start fighting him back. When I heard my thirteen year old brother Sair come from out of his room crying for my dad to stop, that was what made me start fighting harder. I couldn't watch let my brother watch me get raped. I was fighting to the death. He started fumbling with his jeans as I clawed at his face. "Get the fuck up off of me!" I yelled.

"Nah bitch, you want to be grown? Imma show you grown!"

As I continued to wrestle with him, I saw my Mom coming from behind him holding a butchers knife. "Fuck you Mike! I fucking hate you!" She yelled right before she stabbed him in his back. He rolled off of me just as my Mom brought the knife back down in his stomach. She had snapped and as she continued to stab him, I crawled into a corner in the living-room as the severity of what I just happened and what could've happened became a reality. I watched my dad who had just attempted to rape me, take his last breath as the blade of the knife exited and reentered his body.

I was in a daze when I heard bamming on the front door. I sat completely still as my Mother continued to stab my father's lifeless body. When the front door came crashing in and two uniformed police officers rushed in with their guns drawn, I just sat there with tears in my eyes.

"M'am please drop your weapon. Everything is ok, just please put the knife down."

My Mom drop to her knees clutching her stomach as blood started oozing down her legs. Sair rushed to her side with tears free falling from his eyes. She was yelling out in pain as the white officer put her in handcuffs.

"Call an ambulance!" I yelled as the officers pulled her to her feet. The blood was now running like a faucet down her leg and I was scared that she was about to miscarry the baby. The black officer asked for a bus in his walkie talkie as they attempted to calm my Mom down.

"The ambulance is three minutes away, everything will be ok. Will you be able to tell me what has gone on here m'am?" Asked the white police officer. He looked like he was more interested in the crime scene then my Mom's health.

"I… I don't give a fuck about what has gone on here!" My Mom said, huffing and puffing. "Just get me into the fucking ambulance and get these fucking cuffs off of me!"

I heard the sirens of the fire truck and ambulance getting closer to our apartment as I said a quick prayer to God to get my Mom and brother through this. Once the ambulance came inside our apartment and put my Mom up on the gurney, something in my heart told me everything would be okay.

In the back of the ambulance, we flew through the streets at top speed to get my Mom to the hospital. I held on to my Moms hand tightly as the EMT attempted to stop the bleeding. My Mom's face was contorted up in pain as she felt the baby losing consciousness in her womb. "Please hurry up, I can feel the baby suffocating! Please help me deliver this baby!" She cried.

As many times as I had seen my Mother cry, none was ever as painful as this. The pain was resonating from her heart and as they attempted to deliver my brother, I closed my eyes and continued to pray that everything would be fine.

They made me wait in the visiting room in the hospital as my Mom gave birth prematurely. She wasn't due for another two months and the chances of my brother surviving were very slim.

I was pacing back and forth the entire time hoping and praying everything would be fine. Hours passed before someone came out of my Mother's delivery room to let me and Sair know that she had delivered a five pound and seven ounce baby.

Tears of joy rolled down my rosy cheeks as I was led into her delivery room. I held on to Sair's hand tightly as we took in our Mother's appearance. She was sleeping with bandages wrapped around her bruised ribs and head. She looked as if she was finally at peace, and when I walked over to my baby brother inside the hospital issued bassinet the water works started.

He was so beautiful and all I could do was thank God that both he and my Mom had pulled through. Our dad was out of the picture and I knew we could finally be out peace.

At least that was what I was thinking when the same white officer who had come to our house came strolling into the room. "Diane Lewis, you are under arrest for the murder of Michael Lee Lewis. You have the right to remain silent. Anything you say can and will be used against you in the court of law. You have the right to an attorney. If you cannot afford an attorney, one will be appointed to you."

My Mom wasn't coherent as he read her her rights and my anger hit an all time high as I got in the officer's face.

"What the fuck do you mean she's under arrest? She killed my father in self-defense and you know it!"

"Get your little black ass out of my face before I lock your ass up too. Your mother is under arrest so sit down and shut the fuck up!"

"Fuck you!" I spat in his face and turned on my heels as he put my mother in handcuffs. *He gone get his,* I thought as I left the hospital without a backwards glance. Leaving Sair alone to fend for himself was the hardest thing I ever had to do, but I knew we'd be reunited. It was fate.

Chapter Two

The Up and Up

These niggas thought just because I was a female they could get over on me! What they didn't know was I am the baddest bitch to ever do it and for their treachery they'd have to be dealt with, I thought, as I sat in the rented Lincoln town car with my twin desert eagles seated in the passengers seat. I was watching the house where the niggas who robbed me stayed, and my trigger finger was itching. *I can't wait to get my shit back,* I thought.

I sat back and thought about what had got me in the position I was in and shook my head. After leaving the hospital I hit the ground hard on a paper chase. I wasn't sure how I would survive with my Mom possibly going to prison so I did what I felt was natural to me. I started hustling. I knew my boyfriend Ju'Tone was heavy in the dope game so I did what I needed to do. I sucked and fuck that nigga so good he was glad to hand over some work for me. By time my mom's trial came up, I had already started my come up. I was living a little better, and I had a few stacks saved and I was counting on my mom getting out so I could take care of her.

I felt as if I was having an out of body experience when they handed my Mom eight years for voluntary manslaughter. Although the bruises she and I had endured and showed, the judge felt as if killing my father wasn't enough of a punishment. He wanted her to suffer for a little while. My Mother mouthed to me that she'd be okay as she was led out of the courtroom. I knew she would be, but who I was really worried about was my baby brother. He would be lost in the system because I wasn't old enough to take care of him. I left the courthouse a brand new woman. Cash and vengeance was the only things I thought about from that day on.

The day the niggas robbed me for my shit was the day I became a full-fledged hustler, and I guess I was going to have to show these niggas I went just as hard as any nigga. *Maybe harder!*

I had been watching that house for about four hours waiting to make my move. Word around the hood was that the niggas who robbed me for my shit lived inside the house. Ju'Tone wanted to send some of his goons to retrieve his shit but I assured him everything would be taken care of. Grabbing both of my guns I clicked the safety off them both. Twisting the silencers on them, I was ready to get it popping. Just as I was about to hop out of the car my phone began buzzing. *Fuck!* I thought as I answered.

"Hello?" I answered with major attitude.

"Bitch, what the fuck is you doing?" My girl Lola replied, sounding extra ghetto.

"I'm kind of busy so I'll call you back." I told her trying to rush her off the phone.

"Girl I know you not still tripping over that shit that happened with them niggas. You'll just have to take it as a loss and start over." She began saying.

"Sorry but I didn't ask for your opinion."
Click.

Fuck she mean, 'take it as a loss?' That was eight ounces of coke and ten thousand dollars in cash. Bitch must be out of her mind.

I was overly pissed now and was ready to get this shit over with. Double checking my guns, I hopped out of the car. My 5'7" frame was covered in all black with my honey blonde hair pulled into a bun underneath a ball cap. If anyone was to see me which I doubt being that it was pitch black outside courtesy of the broken street lights and the time, I'd probably look like a teen boy.

Getting to the house, I went around the back to check the windows. Looking inside I could see one of the men who robbed me sitting in the bedroom. He was dumping money and drugs onto the bed as I continued watching him. Just the sight of him made me want to pop him where he stood.

"Man that nigga Ritchie was really holding!" he exclaimed, looking over his shoulder to talk to his partner.

"Damn they got my nigga Ritchie too!" I whispered. *Theses niggas just robbing everybody,* I thought.

Leaving the money on the bed he took the pistol from his waistband and also dropped that onto the bed. Going into the living room, he and the other guy were out of sight. With both guns in my hands I walked to the front of the house. Walking straight up to the front door I let off two rounds into the door and kicked it in.

Bam! The door swung open. Both men were unprepared as I hit the man with braids I seen inside the bedroom with two shots to the chest and two to the dome.

The other man dressed in a wife beater, blue jeans and timberlands was able to dive behind the couch. He let off two shots landing two inches above my head in the wall behind me.

"Stupid mu'fucka!" I yelled as I hit him once between the eyes. His body made a loud thud as I raced into the bedroom. I hurried into the room to get my shit. I grabbed the duffle bag and started putting all the money and drugs dude had put onto the bed back inside the bag. I was dashing out of the room when I dropped a stack of money on the floor. *Jackpot.*

There were more duffle bags underneath the bed. When I opened one, there was nothing but drugs inside. Opening another, there was money inside. Originally I had only come to get what I was owed, but seeing the opportunity I was being handed, I decided to take it all. There were three bags underneath the bed, not counting the bag I already had in my hands.

After three trips to and from the car, I sped away with more money and drugs then I'd ever touched. Once I got home, I sat down and counted all the money I had stolen from their house. After an hour of counting and recounting, I had come up with a *$250,000* in cash without adding the four kilos of coke in the other bags. I stayed up the remainder of the night formulating a plan on how I was going to go from nothing to something overnight. I was on my way to the top!

Gangsta
The Sair Lewis story

Bronchey Sair

Chapter One
It was All A Dream

I listened in horror to the sounds of my mother being beaten by my Dad. I closed my eyes as the tears fell, wishing it would stop.

"Mike I swear I didn't know you'd be here early. The chicken is almost done, just let me go finish it." I heard her cry.

My door was cracked, and every hit, moan, and cry reverberated around my room.

God please help her, I prayed.

When I heard the front door to the cramped apartment we lived in open, I knew God had heard my prayer. Mei'Yari was home and when I heard her yelling at our Dad to stop, I knew things would only get worse.

"Daddy stop! I'm so fucking sick and tired of you coming in here putting your hands on us. How about you just take yo drunk ass somewhere else and leave us the fuck alone!"

He would come home ready to pounce on one of us. I had seen my Mom receive more ass whippings and black eyes then any indication of love that I could remember. There weren't any peaceful moments in the Lewis household and if things didn't change quick, I knew someone was going to end up dead.

"Bitch what the fuck yo lil fast ass say to me?" I knew things were about to get worse, so I walked out of my room as slowly as possible. My Mom's eyes looked from him to me to Mei'Yari as he turned his rage to her.

"No Mei'Yari, it's okay. Just go in your room and everything will be ok." My Mom was pleading with her, but I knew she wouldn't listen.

"No Mom, fuck that! This sorry excuse for a man needs to get the fuck up outta here. I'm tired of this shit!"

"Oh you think you grown now huh? Done started having sex and you think you can say anything you want to me huh?"

I was scared out of my mind.

"Well imma show you just how grown you really are!" I watched my Dad start pulling at her shirt.

Fear paralyzed me as he began pulling her to the ground. It took about a second after he pulled her blouse off her to start fighting him back.

I started crying for my Dad to stop, but my pleas fell upon deaf ears.

My Mom came from out of nowhere with a butchers knife and plunged it as deep as she could into his back. She had finally snapped.

"Fuck you Mike! I fucking hate you!" She yelled right before she stabbed him again.

He rolled off of Mei'Yari leaving his stomach exposed . My Mom brought the knife down into his stomach and as the blood squirted from his insides, I became numb. I was in a daze.

The bamming on the door and the police entering the house did nothing to make me feel safe. My eyes wouldn't leave the lifeless body of my Dad. His eyes were wide open, with no life behind them.

I could hear my Mom yelling in pain as she begun to give birth to the baby she carried in her stomach.

Mei'Yari had to lead me to the ambulance as they attempted to assist my Mom in deliver.

I remained silent as we rode to the hospital. Mei'Yari kept her arms around me the entire time, making me feel as if she'd be here for me forever... At least that's what I thought.

My Mom gave birth to a premature baby boy, and the fact that they survived the trauma my Dad inflicted upon them made me feel as if life would get a little better.

Him being out of our lives was a joyous occasion. Mei'Yari and I entered her room a few hours later to finally catch a look at my Mom and the new addition to our family. She was lying in bed with bandages wrapped around her head.

She finally looked at peace.

Kissing her on the cheek, I walked over to where my baby brother was sleeping, and a tear slid down my eye. He was the spitting image of our father. Mei'Yari stood next to me and looked down at him.

We stood there trying to figure out what his name would be when someone entered the room. Turning around, it was the cop that had come to our home.

"Diane Lewis, you are under arrest for the murder of Michael Lee Lewis. You have the right to remain silent. Anything you say can and will be used against you in the court of law. You have the right to an attorney. If you cannot afford an attorney, one will be appointed to you."

I was confused the entire time he was reading her her rights. Mei'Yari's anger hit an all-time high and she jumped in the officer's face.

"What the fuck do you mean she's under arrest? She killed my father in self-defense and you know it!"

"Get your little black ass out of my face before I lock your ass up too. Your mother is under arrest now so sit down and shut the fuck up!"

"Fuck you!"

She spat in his face and turned on her heels as he put my mother in handcuffs. She left the hospital without a backwards glance and that was the last time I ever saw my sister.

Mei'Yari! Mei'Yari! I pleaded inside my head. But no words were coming out of my mouth. Where was I to go from here! Mei'Yari!

Chapter Two
Pour it Up

I woke up in a cold sweat for the third time this week. I had been having the same nightmare that wasn't really a nightmare, but my past over and over again.

The day my life changed forever seemed to be plaguing me continuously, although I tried my hardest to live for the day and not for yesterday. I didn't want to live for my past, especially today. *My high school graduation.*

The sounds of Miss Emma's slippers gliding across the floor signaled her approach. She knocked on my door twice and entered my room. "Boy are you decent?" She asked, opening the door with her eyes closed.

I chuckled before replying, "Yeah."

"How are you feeling this morning? My little boy is graduating high school today!" A single tear slid down her face. I had been with Miss Emma practically since the day my family split apart in the hospital.

Right after Mei'Yari turned her back on me and my Mom was carted off to jail leaving me abandoned in the hospital, Miss Emma found me and took me in.

She had been in the hospital with her husband who was recovering from surgery when she found me crying. She was never able to have kids of her own so after finding me and taking me in, I became the son she always wanted.

"Don't cry ma. You raised me well, I'm just growing up. Don't cry at the graduation either!"

"Boy shut up, I'll cry if I want too!" We burst into laughter. "When you finally get up, go out to the mailbox for me."

"I'm up, so I can go right now."

She exited my room, and I hopped out of the bed. I heard the front door closing but paid it no mind.

Why she want me to check the mail if she going outside? I thought.

The reoccurring dream had me ready to do anything to occupy my thoughts until graduation.

I put my black *Nike* slippers on my feet and headed outside to check the mailbox. Turning the corner of the house to go down the driveway, I was greeted by my parents yelling "surprise!"

They were standing in front of a glossy black 2013 Mercedes Benz G Wagon truck. A huge grin spread across my face. "This me? For real," I asked, unbelievingly.

"Yeah Sair, this is your car. You deserve it and we just wanted to show you how proud we are of you. The day you came into our lives has been one of the best things that could've happened to us. Congratulations on your big day son!" Mr. Joe was never the sentimental type, but to hear those words come out of his mouth and the single tear that slid out of his eye touched me.

Never feeling love from my own father made my relationship with Mr. Joe that much stronger.

"Thanks dad!" They both embraced me and it felt good to feel loved.

"I know you dying to take it for a spin, cut loose!" He said, putting the keys in my hand.

"I am, but I can wait until after I get dressed for graduation. Then I will!" I laughed. "But thank you mom and dad. You guys don't understand just how much you both mean to me and I appreciate everything you've ever done for me."

My Mom started bawling, wrapping her arms around me again. "I love you so much Sair!"

"I love you too."

After all the dramatics, they reentered the house, leaving me outside to admire my new wheels. I took a seat on the black leather and inhaled the new car smell. I was overly juiced as I pulled on the steering wheel, envisioning myself on the streets cutting loose.

Yeah this graduation need to hurry up, I thought.

Lounging around the house for a few hours watching HBO's newest show *Billionaire Boyz* based on the novel by Bronchey Battle. The show was crazy and I loved it. The chick they had playing Saniya was a dime.

The show stayed true to the book, which was a hood classic that I had in my library. I watched a few episodes of that until eleven so I could turn up.

Black *Levi's* were on my ass, paired with wheat colored *Timberlands* on my feet. A bleached denim shirt graced my upper body. Buttoned completely to the top, a half-black, half-wheat colored bowtie around my neck.

A gold wishbone chain lay nestled underneath. My jet black curls sat atop my head with a part on the left side. My butterscotch complexion, dark brown eyes, light goatee and neck tattoos were the females *drugs of choice* around the way.

I was ready to get the show on the road, so I grabbed my cap 'n gown out of my closet and met my parents in the living room.

"Look at you!" My Mom said, when she saw me. "It's a photo shoot!" She said, snapping pictures.

"Dang ma, let me pose first!"

My dad started cracking up as I did my poses. "Aha, you a mess boy."

"Come hop in some of these dad." He got in the pictures and we started cutting up. He got down on the ground, crossed his arms and started mugging the camera. I couldn't help but laugh. "Doing them 1987 poses!"

"These was the ones back in the day!" he replied.

"Dad take some of me and Mom."

They switched places and I wrapped my arm around my Mom. I stood at 6'3" towering over her who stood at 5'6". Her beautiful dark brown skin, short haircut and perfect white teeth were amazing. Miss Emma was definitely a looker. Mr. Joe, brown skin, standing at 6'0" was smooth, with an undeniable swag that I'm sure had the hoes falling head over heels for him back in the day.

They were a stunning couple who were madly in love. I only hoped I found a love like there's one day.

I took a couple pictures by my ride to post on instagram before getting behind the wheel to head to the *Concord Pavilion. Toot It and Boot It* by YG featuring Ty Dolla Sign blared out of the speakers of the two fifteens in the trunk.

I cruised the freeway with my parents following behind in their white 2013 Tesla. I glanced in my rearview mirror every now and them to check on them as I accelerated to see what my baby could do.

Grabbing the white grape *Splitarillo* filled with *purple kush*, I lit it and blew one on the freeway.

I had definitely lucked up the day Miss Emma found me in the hospital. With her being a retired nurse and Mr. Joe owning several successful businesses including a luxury car dealership, they were sitting on paper.

I never wanted for anything, although the material things didn't matter to me. The thing that they gave me that I cherished the most was love and a chance.

A chance to become *SOMEONE* in this world. With their help and blessing, I'm on my way to becoming an entertainment lawyer headed to *Howard University.*

Pulling into the parking lot of the *Concord Pavilion*, I turned heads. Some of the females I went to school with came flocking towards my truck after I put it in park.

"This you?" Asked this brown skin cutie named Konnie.

"Yup, grad present from the folks!"

"It's nice. Almost look as good as you," she winked. Shit like that happened to me on a regular.

"Thank you gorgeous."

My Mom took a picture of us, than we headed inside for the ceremony. It was scorching inside my burgundy cap 'n gown.

The ceremony seemed to draw on for awhile. When they reached the L's, it was time for me to head to the stage. I was waiting for my name to be called with the most confidence displayed across my face.

"Sair Lewis!" Everyone started screaming for me.

I couldn't help but to start cheesing when the crowd went crazy. All my niggas hopped up for me as I grabbed my diploma. I noticed my Mom yelling the loudest while wiping tears out of her eyes. I took a bow on stage, took a photo with the Principal and went to my seat.

I was overly hyped. I had done it!

The highlight of the graduation had to be when they called "Sophe Si."

Walking across the stage, she ripped open her green cap 'n gown. Underneath her gown, she exposed an outfit that was imitated from the *Sun Drop* soda commercials. She started dancing and I started cracking up.

"Ayyyyyyyyyyeeeeeeee!" Everybody started cheering.

She snatched her diploma and had the entire pavilion in laughter. I stood on top of a chair and started yelling for my nigga. The security had to come over and ask me to have a seat.

I tuned the remainder of the ceremony out up until my principal started a speech to conclude the graduation.

"... Today is the beginning of your life as adults. Always be responsible for what you say and do. You are now headed into adulthood. You now have responsibilities to own every decision you make in your Life for this moment on. Always think before you act. Congratulations to *MT. Diablo High, class of '12*. Let's give a huge hand to Sair Lewis for his signing to *Howard University*. Make us proud. I am very proud of each and every one of you!" Ms. Gooch, concluded.

She raised her hand and motioned for us to stand. In response, we threw our hats into the air, yelling and screaming, happy to be free of high school.

In front of the pavilion I flicked it up with everyone that I was cool with. After about a million pictures, I was free to go. It was party time. No more high school, just big dreams, parties, and women!

Pour it up, Pour it up, that's how we ball out.

Exquisite Nights

An Erotic Tale of
Two Sisters

Bronchey Ju'Tone Sair

Chapter One

Nemiah

"You looked amazing at the club tonight!" Jacob, complimented, as he pulled me into his embrace.

"Thanks babe. You know I dedicated my entire set to you" I said, running my right hand the length of his face.

"Is that right?" He asked in his soft baritone.

"Yes," I whispered seductively into his ear as I unbuttoned the white sheer blouse I wore. He stuck his tongue down my throat as his hands roamed my body.

"Damn," I moaned, with my right hand unbuttoning the belt to the slacks he wore.

"You want to feel it?" he asked, looking me in the eyes.

Nodding my head up and down, I grabbed his dick in the palm of my hands. "Can I taste it daddy?" I asked, licking his earlobe.

"YES!"

Getting from his lap, I positioned myself on my knees. Sliding down the *Tom Ford* slacks, I grabbed for his dick that was sticking out the hole of the briefs he wore.

My tongue grazed the head as I kept my eyes locked to Jacob's. I began circling the head and he started clenching his toes. Inch by inch entered my mouth as I took as much as I could of him down my throat.

"Oh my GOODNESS!" He moaned loudly, grabbing the back of my head. He slowly started grinding into my mouth while keeping a firm hand on my head.

"Does your wife do that for you?" I asked, putting on an award worthy performance.

"No," replied, shaking his head. "I want to be inside you my beautiful African Queen."

I rolled my eyes on the sly as he made his statement.

Getting up, Jacob pushed me onto the bed, lying on my stomach. Using his left hand, he lifted me up by my waist to give an arch in my back.

Removing a condom out of his wallet, he ripped it open and slid it on his dick. Turning my head to face him as he began to enter my flood gates, I took in the man penetrating me.

Standing at 6'1", he had a stocky build. A neatly trimmed goatee that had specks of gray showing. Tan white skin, with blue eyes.

"Put it in me Daddy," I moaned as he slid his seven inches in me. "AHHHH SHIT!"

"You feel me?" He asked, stroking me slowly.

"YESSSSS," I replied, throwing it back at him. Our rhythm began to build and he attempted to beat it up. The sounds of skin smacking reverberated around the room as we went at it.

"This is AMAZING," he moaned. His hands were on my waist as he thrust himself inside of me. Sweat had begun to form and I could feel he was close to coming already.

"Lay on the bed Jacob, I want to ride it!"

Pulling out of me slowly, he positioned himself at the head of the bed. Before taking my position on top of him, I grabbed the remote to the surround sound and turned it on.

Pussy by Chris Brown serenaded us as I crawled seductively towards Jacob. Once I reached his lap, I slid him inside me and rode him to the beat of the song.

"I'm about to CU- CUUUM!" he moaned.

His dick got rock hard before he bust. He lay stiff as a board as he shot his load into the condom.

"That was good babe," he said, slightly panting out of breath.

"How good?" I asked, kissing his lips.

"Go grab the roll of money out of my slacks and that's your answer.

Dollar signs appeared in my eyes as I raced off the bed to retrieve the slacks off the floor of the hotel suite. Pulling the knot of money out of his pocket, I slid it inside the white vintage Chanel bag I entered the suite with.

"You aren't going to count it?" He asked, with his left arm nestled behind his head.

"Nah," I replied, strutting with the precision of a model into the huge bathroom. Turning on the water, I stepped inside to let the steam cascade down my body.

A gust of wind hit my back, and the closing of the shower door let me know Jacob had joined me.

His hands were roaming my body as I let the water play in my kinky straight hair that hung to the middle of my back.

"Can I wash your back?" He asked, head resting on my shoulder.

"Yeah, but I just forgot I left my wash in the room, I'll be right back."

"OK, I'll be here when you get back."

I hopped out of the shower and headed towards my Chanel bag. Grabbing the silver plated .25 out of it, I clicked the safety off.

Grabbing the remote to the surround system, I turned its volume to the max. Stepping into the black leggings and sheer blouse I wore, I was dressed in a matter of seconds. I entered the bathroom just as Jacob stuck his head out the shower. Before he knew it, a bullet had entered his forehead.

Sick motha'fucka!

I immediately wiped down any and everything I may have touched in the room. I was like a chicken with my head cut off. Grabbing my purse, I rushed the hotel leaving another body in my wake.

Coming Soon!